CURRENT-RIPPED ON CAPE LOOKOUT

CAPE POINTE BOOK 2

By Cindy M. Amos

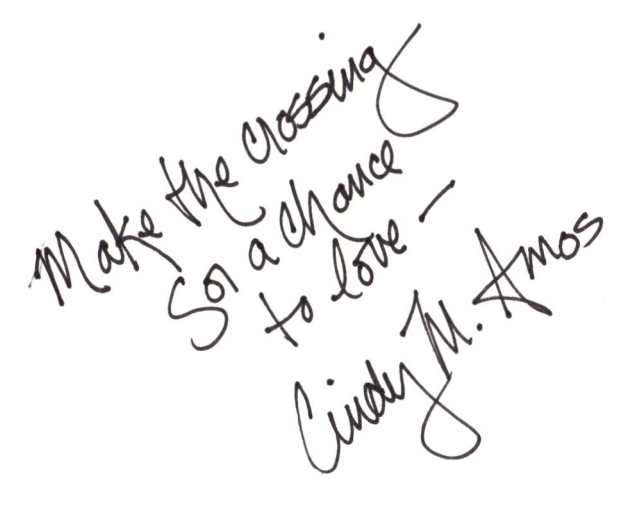

Make the crossing for a chance to love —

Cindy M. Amos

Copyright © 2021 by Cindy M. Amos
Published by Forget Me Not Romances, an imprint of Winged Publications

This book is a work of fiction. Names, characters, places, and incidents are the product of the author's imagination and are used fictitiously. Any resemblance to actual events, locales, or persons, living or dead, is coincidental.

All rights reserved including the right to reproduce this book or portions thereof in any form whatsoever – except short passages for reviews – without express permission.

ISBN: 9798532642560

*For nothing harbored in secret can remain,
but will become evident to all;
neither is the hidden matter safe,
but will become as clear as daylight.
Luke 18:17*

Dedicated to:
Core Bankers who loved the middle cape
and left dune buggies on its golden sands.

Acknowledgments:
Cameron H. Amos, Original Cover Design
Cynthia Hickey, Winged Publications
Stacey Rogers, Trinity Social Media

Chapter 1

She'd started too late for this journey, a fact the racing current made ever apparent. Shaina Gillespie adjusted her footing to keep the stand-up paddleboard from nosing directly into the rippling stream forced by the bottom of an ebbing tide. At this rate, Core Sound would decant into the mighty Atlantic Ocean with her riding escort. Over her shoulder, Cape Lookout wagged a sandy finger of correction, as she'd vowed to her mother to keep her SUP on inland waters.

Curse the promise that can't be kept. She shifted forward, hoping to dig the nose of the board under the surface and brake against the misdirecting flow. Drawn seaward at a steady clip, she'd never make her destination, the beachfront of Shackleford Banks. With the paddle as her only weapon, she stroked at a rapid pace until her shoulders ached. Crossing the ebb current proved impossible. Between two land masses, she floundered against the water's command.

When the half-sunken war bunker came into sight, a chill shot down her spine offsetting the heat of June. Though no German U-boats awaited her tiny vessel, the ocean had no shortage of other perils to offer. From the outer shore, wave action could make a beach landing more like a Normandy invasion of the personal kind. Seconds ticked by as the tide drew out the sound's contents through the narrow inlet between the two islands.

She lost traction with her lead foot, shortening her next breath. Though she'd perfected paddleboarding for over a year, her confidence took wing with the slipping motion to alight on a distant shore. Her knees started to quiver. With a broad sweep to turn the board's nose back toward Lookout, she could abort the mission. The current volleyed against the move and turned her ever south—straight to the mouth of Barden's Inlet where she'd never dared to go.

The upper corner of the concrete bunker scarred Lookout's scenic island vista to her left. Remnant from less peaceable times, the bunker held few prisoners in its day. Sunk in the sand, the structure seemed poised to be claimed by the sea at any given moment. Should the narrow inlet shift in a hurricane, that swallow-up might happen.

The current dipped in a small trough as a standing wave formed from the fluid motion constricting past the sandy shores of both islands. Shaina chose the closest beach to focus on, her last chance to clasp land before being dragged out to sea. She knelt on the board, secured the paddle between her knees, and alternately cupped water in her hands trying to make for the protruding spit of sand on the Shackleford side.

Rough waters shook her floating platform in the crossing. A huge mullet leapt from the water and splashed her as if racing to the inlet. All at once, the board began to quake, dipping side to side. To lessen the tempest, she lowered to her stomach. Every ripple turned gigantic with her new perspective. Panicked, she dug deeper beneath the water's surface, attempting a last-ditch maneuver out of harm's way until her shoulder muscles burned.

A dark cloud of thunderous motion split the dune line over on Shackleford Banks. A herd of galloping wild ponies crossed the ridge aimed straight for the water's edge. Distracted in the moment, she failed to navigate the next hazard, the convergence of two currents running parallel to each shore. She lasted half an inhalation when the board struck her forehead and then bucked her into the labyrinth.

Cool sound waters closed over her as she sank like an unwitting submarine. A modern U-boat with no mission to accomplish, she clung to the paddleboard in white-knuckled fear while her skull throbbed with pain. *Survive to tell about it.* She surfaced, but the current splashed her face, causing her to gag. Braced against the board, she grew powerless to navigate the onslaught.

~

Judd Pearce felt his sunset ride shift from glorious to gut-wrenching as the woman with shapely legs fell from her paddleboard and dipped into the sound. He'd ridden to the shore on Thunder, a well-padded stallion that assumed the herd's lead when the gray-muzzled Atlantica succumbed two months ago. The herd had experienced a scattershot of deaths since then, which confused his scientific research even further.

To slow the heaving pony, he slipped a hand down the side of its harness. As the dwarfed beast descended the primary dune line, he slid from its back and hit the beachfront running. Before he could wade into the sound thigh-deep, the woman lost her last handhold on the paddleboard and disappeared from sight. Not willing to let the day lapse into full-fledged tragedy, he dove toward her and swam at an angle to offset the swift current.

Intercepting the nose of the paddleboard first, he maneuvered around its length and caught a stretchy cord across his arm. As he fished for the far end, he took a deep inhalation and prepared to dive. Before he could register the meaning, a slender ankle filled his palm. Next, he spotted the wrapped floral print of the woman's board shorts, so he reeled her in like an ensnared fish, hand over hand, wrapping the cord around his wrist.

The woman's eyes fluttered open for a moment, a flash of honey-brown. "No ocean."

He spied the tip of Shackleford's sandy shoal as it passed on his right. Unfettered by the land mass, the paddleboard made for the open ocean with total abandon. To avoid the ocean excursion, he would have to force the woman and her vessel toward the shore. Using a strong dolphin kick, he thrust his shoulder landward and pressed the issue in his preferred direction.

As if entertained by his sputtering performance,

the ponies followed along the intertidal zone and trailed out onto the sandy spit, an interactive audience. Though provoked to laugh, he couldn't spare the breath. He managed two more kicks when the woman hooked her elbow around his neck and trailed behind, streamlining his efforts. With the board bobbing from the far end of the cord, he bested the ripping current and soon landed in the shallows.

Stormy, the best swimmer in the herd, nickered not far from his position. Taken as an offer to help, he redirected for the four-hoofed assistant. The pony waded out to shoulder height, its head elevated with wary jerks. The whites of its dark eyes flashed with alarm.

"Steady, boy." He eased the woman onto the pony's back and gestured for the shore. When his hand dropped back into the water, he caught a length of ankle leash. A necessary detachment, he yanked the Velcro closure loose from her leg and took sole possession of the paddleboard. Lacking any exposure to this type of leisure craft, he settled for splaying across its length and paddling to shore in low profile.

Stormy halted just short of the wrack line from the afternoon's high tide where the victim slid off in a fetal curl onto the drying sand. A moan accompanied the shift which caused the herd to back away. A herring gull abandoned the beach with a complaining cry at the disturbance.

Judd floated the board as far as it would go. When sand scraped the bottom, he rolled off into the shallows and rose onto his knees. Beyond the woman, only a six-foot stretch of sand had prevented the inevitable meet-up with the mighty Atlantic Ocean, a slender success. "Not today, Neptune." With a shove landward, the paddleboard's shallow skegs gripped Shackleford Banks with some degree of permanence.

He soon knelt beside the victim to assess her medical condition. *Finally, an advantage.* A darkening lump on her right temple spelled head trauma, though he didn't know how severe. At best calculation, the cot inside his tent offered softer accommodation than water-lain sand. Without much of a jostle, he scooped her up in his arms and rose to make quick work of the journey back to research central. As a specimen, she resembled more of a mermaid than his typical equine client which would make for an interesting recovery period.

~

Shaina awoke with a throbbing headache to find a sunburned hippie with overgrown whiskers staring down at her by lantern light. She scanned the olive-green canvas roof that vaulted in the center of the room. "Where am I?"

"Pearce Research Center on the east end of Shackleford Banks. We don't get many drop-in guests out here, so welcome to our humble facility. How's the head?"

"Feels like the size of a pigmy sperm whale, and white-hot at that. Did you pull me from the ocean?"

He drew closer which sparked a twinkle in his brown eyes. "No, when the struggling paddleboarder said *no ocean*, I tried my best to keep that destination from happening. Note the outgoing current worked dead against that notion." A pony neighed from somewhere close by.

A bit of clarity returned. "I saw a wild pony in the water—or was I dreaming?"

"Yes, you did. That's Stormy. He's young and foolhardy. I'll introduce you tomorrow."

"What? Is it too late for me to go back to Lookout?"

"Yes, too late for today. You've already proven how treacherous those inlet currents can be. Lacking any visual cues at night, the crossing turns much too risky." He stepped away and stirred something behind him with a soothing metallic scrape.

The aroma of food caused her stomach to join her head in complaint mode. She tried to sit up with a grunt. The room began to spin clockwise with the tent's center pole at the axis. Instead of fighting the sensation, she relaxed her shoulders and accepted her fate as a shipwrecked foundling. "Do you have a first name, Mr. Pearce?"

"Uh, that's Doctor Pearce actually." He shifted back to face her. "Judson Pearce, DVM. My friends, associates, and other miscellaneous mermaids collected on the beach call me Judd." A slight smile dug into his tanned cheek.

She touched the tape pulling at her eyebrow. "I'm getting medical help from a vet?"

"Minor frontal contusion. No blood. Cold pack administered until you melted the last bit of ice I had saved." His gaze swept her torso as if in brief assessment. "I held off on the horse liniment, but if you're sore, I can apply some at your direction."

She blew out a breath in surrender. "No, thank you. Just let me stay here without moving my head. I'd like to stave off that explosion." Her stomach rumbled next—a real traitor.

"And what of your pending implosion from wanton hunger?" The question seemed to brush across his funny bone as his half-cocked smile returned.

"I'm fully captive in your galley. What's for dinner?"

"Hot pork and beans with some clams I dug from the marsh last night. They're rubbery, but filling. Can I ask your name?"

"I'm Shaina Gillespie. Guess I'll choke down a few clams as opposed to endless chewing. I need to keep my head as motionless as possible."

"I tried to explain that exact point to Stormy when he wanted to carry you here to my tent. For some reason, he thought we were playing finders keepers out on the beach." He chuckled and leaned closer. "In all seriousness, Shaina, I need to prop you up so you can swallow some sustenance. Be a sweet patient and help me get this sleeping bag shoved behind you." He held out a brawny forearm. "Grab hold and pull forward, if you can."

She placed her hands on his arm and felt him flinch. "I've heard mermaids are fussy and uncooperative." She bent at the waist and tried to hold the pose while he pried the roll into position behind her. When she eased back, the adjustment set off a massive temple throb for a few heartbeats, causing her next snarky comment to fizzle before she could render it.

Judd produced a shallow pan full of simmered beans. "See, you don't act like a mermaid. Besides, I looked you up in my field guide to indigenous island species. You possess two legs, so you're neither an island glass lizard nor a mermaid. A generalist, I'm lumping you into the category of a large animal species and can treat your symptoms accordingly. Now, blow on this spoonful as it's still pretty hot."

The way he'd emphasized *pretty* caused her lashes to flutter. A mouthful of beans came accentuated by both bacon and maple flavors. Outside the realm of ordinary, she gave the room a quick inspection as she chewed the morsel. A shelf of sample jars topped a messy desk area. After she swallowed, she had to delve. "So what exactly are you studying?"

"The ponies. That's the long and short of it. I have an anonymous sponsor who doesn't want any further information leaked, so I'll leave my answer at that. Here, try the clams. I sautéed them in olive oil, so you can't say I didn't try to make them palatable."

She ate one off his fork and started to chew. Rubber cement would have been less challenging. After a prolonged effort that set off her head throb again, she capitulated and swallowed the remaining lump. "Garlic would help that dish, Doctor DVM."

"Garlic ran out my second week camping over here, along with the onion. I spilled all the salt into a clambake pot, which made for a wretched batch of leftovers. Even the blue crabs down by the dock refused to partake. I only have a bit of turmeric left, all the more reason to pull up stakes next week and return to civilization. I need to start writing up my research, anyway."

She accepted another bite of beans before growing introspective. Beholden for the rescue, the need to equal matters out nudged her into action. "Say you'll come to my side of the inlet for a hot dinner prior to shipping back to the mainland. I want to express my gratitude for saving me from breaking my pledge to my mother not to venture out into the ocean alone."

"Aha, a broken pledge salvaged at the last possible second." His brow rose with intrigue. "And how might I accomplish this crossing of Core Sound to receive your reciprocation? You'll possess the paddleboard—and I lack any boat."

"Well, how did you plan to leave Shackleford Banks?"

"The park service has partnered with my sponsor to ferry me and my supplies back to the mainland on our agreed-upon date." He offered another fork-load of clams looking slightly mysterious.

"Then I suggest you ride Stormy across the inlet at dead low tide. The currents will subside by then. Come over Monday afternoon before hide tide pushes through the inlet. I'll be ready to show off *my* research project—packing up the lighthouse keeper's quarters for relocation to the mainland."

The empty fork slipped from his hand, his expression embattled.

"Is that a yes? Will you come to dinner on

Monday, Dr. Pearce?"

He glanced down as though a marauding ghost crab had scuttled into the tent. "We'll be there. As for Stormy, he'll be delighted to learn he's being included."

"Tell Stormy that I'm switching his finders-keepers antics to a playful game of island tag." To prove she was no longer *it* as an owing victim, she swatted the good doctor's forearm.

He stared at the point of contact. "Your dinner seems to heighten the stakes a notch."

"Yes, heightened stakes. After all, I have the lighthouse on my island. That ups the ante a bit." Expectant, she allowed him to deliver the next spoonful of beans, complete with a tidbit of bacon. She hummed in response, relinquishing to his unexpected safe harbor until the tidal cycle—and a good night's rest—could eradicate the swollen lump on her head.

She leaned back onto the soft bed roll, wearied from paddling and stricken by the drowsy urge to sleep. When her eyelids shuttered closed, the current ripped at her again. A glimpse of crumpled cotton put the motion mystery to immediate rest as the doctor's caring hand smoothed a sheet against her bare shoulders. A single scrape of the spoon along the pan's bottom led her into an embayment of unconsciousness where she finally made the successful crossing.

Chapter 2

Judd waded onto shore, the weight of false pretense making his gait drag. In his dreams, he'd longed for the freedom availing itself at tonight's dinner invitation by an attractive woman. Since accepting the dubious research assignment last December, all such hopes and dreams became shipwrecked forfeitures, a marine catastrophe for a man wanting so much more.

He exhaled, fixating on the diamond-spackled lighthouse up ahead on the interior of Cape Lookout. The keeper's house would have to be close by, although he'd never ventured this far from his assigned outpost on Shackleford Banks. As if sharing his unease, Stormy nuzzled his arm to prompt him forward.

Plenty warm for early June, he gave the sun another minute to dry his skin. Once he'd fished the T-shirt out of his waterproof pack, he knocked away a few pesky flies and walked through a patch of glasswort before finding a footpath through the marshy fringe. A meadow opened beyond that, where Stormy paused to sample the abundant grass.

The rusted-out carcass of a vehicle made its way

behind the sand dunes rolling toward the keeper's complex. A row of wooden cabins connected by a boardwalk extended north of the ancient maritime structure, looking considerably newer. The park service still had ongoing activities on Cape Lookout, though the Coast Guard had pulled out decades ago.

Unease filled his senses. He pulled the shirt over his head and wrestled his arms into the sleeves. Shaina hadn't mentioned the possibility of any other company at dinner. Somehow, that threat made him rue the occasion even more. With Stormy waylaid by the grass, he slowed his pace and aimed for a stand of wax myrtle shrubs to gain cover.

The vehicle crept to a halt beside the keeper's house. The horn blew with a shrill blast. Beyond the house, a flock of seagulls took wing along the beachfront. Unable to spot the vast blue horizon of the Atlantic Ocean yet, he considered shimmying up the sturdiest myrtle to gain a better vantage point. Within seconds, Shaina appeared on the rear porch and gave an animated wave to the driver. Judd held his breath until the vehicle inched away from the structure. It banked toward him, circled around, and disappeared up the northern stretch of the island.

Stormy joined him with a snort. A shake of its mane sent half a dozen flies swarming for a new host. Inpatient in the glade, the pony pawed at the sand.

"Okay, big boy. Let's go make one colossal mistake, all for the sake of eating a decent meal." He stepped around the shrub thicket and headed straight for the house, the pony ever trailing. Now out in the open, mere seconds passed before Shaina waved one arm over her head to lure him in. "Don't regret this evening, Pearce, you shallow scoundrel." He waved back, soon outdistanced by the Shackleford steed that had broken into a trot.

The uneven hem of Shaina's dress played devil's advocate against the sea breeze, hiding and then revealing her shapely legs. When Stormy nickered, she descended the steps seemingly intent to meet him on level ground. She laughed and welcomed the pony with open arms.

Judd stopped just short of the vehicle tracks and took in the affectionate scene. With the lighthouse in the background, he contemplated whether the keeper had ever tended livestock inside the compound. Lost in languished thought, he must have appeared hesitant.

The hostess gathered the hem of her dress in her hand and stepped toward him. "Hello, Dr. Pearce. Thank you for braving the crossing to accept my dinner invitation. I hope you won't miss your own humble mess hall for one evening."

He shook his head. "There's nothing left over on my side but empty tin cans. I'm all packed up to make the transition back to the mainland in the morning. That lends tonight even more noteworthy commemoration, though I almost didn't make the inlet crossing."

"Well, that makes you a brave man in yet another way, doesn't it?"

"More hungry than courageous, truth be told. Who was driving the old salt-trap of a dune buggy?" He jutted his thumb up the island.

"That's my ride over to the mainland. Gibbs Salter runs a ferry service over to Core Banks for day-trippers. It's for pedestrian traffic only. He keeps that old rolling relic by the dock on the sound side to save a few steps. Gibbs likes to say goodbye before departing. Plus, honking the horn gives the beachgoers ample warning to run for the ferry." She smiled and tucked a loose tendril back into her sculpted top-knot.

"What about the park service?"

"Day duty only, except the contracted team doing sea turtle conservation work out here nightly. We're well into nesting season, though the egg-layers are vanishing from these shores."

"I've read that's a common trend along the Carolina coast over the past few decades. It might help if we keep our lighting to a minimum for dinner tonight."

"As romantic as that sounds, good doctor, I've already made a pact with Cheryl and Jan, the turtle patrol gals, that they won't see an artificial light from my place after sundown. Anyway, next week we're detaching all the plumbing and electrical ties to Mother Earth so the structure can be freed up for transport. Soon, the hunched profile of the keeper's quarters will be erased from the island's horizon, and only the monolith of the lighthouse will remain."

He clapped his hands together, stimulated at the prospect. "I hope to get a grand tour of how that relocation might transpire." When she hesitated, he waggled his brow to add sincerity.

"All in good time, Dr. Pearce. But first, I want

to introduce my pony rescuer to our herbivore's nirvana." She placed her hand on the animal's halter and began to step along a path that circled beyond the lighthouse.

Amused at her special treatment, he had to jockey for position. "Should I tag along?"

"By all means. Only part of the treat is meant for Stormy." She gave a shy smile which hinted of something more.

He strode to catch up and soon allowed the lighthouse's shadow to encompass their threesome. How many men had found shelter in that narrow band of shade on a hot summer's day? He studied the encrusted corrosion around the beacon's heavy-set door as they passed, uninterested in exploring beyond the forbidding portal.

A path opened nearby along a meadow of sea ox-eye, its dainty yellow flowers dotting the sandy landscape. Wide enough to allow him to walk along the pony's opposite flank, he joined the leader. Within steps, he caught his first glimpse of the Atlantic. "Oh, good. Nobody moved the ocean without my knowledge."

"No, it looks the same as it did six years ago. I lived over here planting an experimental plot for my professor when I was a marine science major. I switched to architecture after that summer, but still hold Cape Lookout with particular fondness."

"Aha, so you may have something to do with this Garden of Eden you're luring young Stormy towards. Suddenly, this feels like a trap." He rubbed the equine's front shoulder in commiseration of the unknown.

"Only if entrapment looks the same as a reward." She gestured with a sweep of her hand as tall dunes appeared flanking cape pointe. Teased by a gentle breeze, the thick stand of grass clustered between dunes undulated like a colony of sea anemones along a coral reef.

Idyllic in every way, Judd admired the pristine scene. Pure unspoiled beachfront lay ahead beyond the dune line. Regret that the neighboring island couldn't claim the same soon twisted a tourniquet around his neckband. *Poison always rises.*

"Well, what do you think about my Ammophila grass stabilization planting?" When she freed her hand from the halter, Stormy trotted off to graze, a ringing endorsement.

"Perhaps you have a knack for stabilization, Ms. Gillespie, which may serve you well when floating a monstrous house balanced on a flat barge across tempestuous Core Sound."

"Could you please call me Shaina?"

"Only if we can toss aside the formality of Dr. Pearce, too."

She turned from watching the pony to gaze straight at him. "Does it make me a mermaid to call you Judd?"

He couldn't stop the smile at her association. "No, we've ruled that out. And I don't think any mermaid could pull off wearing that dress. By the way, accept my commendation on your grassy patch. It likely anchored cape pointe when intermittent nor'easters threatened."

"This patch of American beach grass may be a small success in the grand scheme of things, but it means something significant to me."

"I agree. And it's much more natural than that concrete bunker left from the big war. Thank you for starting our tour here. I doubt Stormy will advance much further, given his vigor for your scrumptious beach grass."

She walked past him, headed back up the trail. "Our dinner should be the next order of business then. If Stormy doesn't come find us later, we'll search for him by lantern light."

The allusion of searching the vast island with such a small implement birthed wanderlust of romantic proportion. He followed her back through the sea ox-eye patch, her dress hem undulating like the Ammophila. *Such a stabilizing sway.* A faint yearning mingled with his growing hunger, morphing him into a sojourner he scarcely recognized, a man bearing tender feelings and heightened appreciation for beach grass.

~

Shaina traced the lines of seashells decorating the front porch railing. All Atlantic whelk shells, the falling tide seemed to offer a new specimen for her collection almost daily. Sturdy coils with bony knobs around the apex, she often fingered the smooth peach-colored surface of the animal's aperture, the glasswork of nature. She would miss the view from this platform when the structure found a home plot on the mainland. "Have you read about the dissention between Morehead City and Harkers Island regarding the proper placement of the keeper's house? The issue has sparked quite a competition which the local newspaper loves to fan."

Judd glanced at her over his last forkful of apple tart. "Oh, yes, I'm familiar. You didn't mention the underdog in the three-way fight for possession—my hometown of Beaufort. The keeper's quarters would match the other federal-period houses preserved on our two-acre historic site. I believe there's a grassy plot available right beside the apothecary, as a matter of fact."

She eyed her chatty dinner guest in a new light, given his awareness of the situation. "Morehead City has offered to pay for the relocation costs, though the state historical society has allocated the funding. Their proposed landing site seems too urban for my liking, though."

"So you're favoring Harkers Island then?" His brow rose with the question as he devoured the remaining bite of apple tart.

"Progress always arrives in slow motion for Harkers Island. They have a real knack for holding onto tradition and the old ways of coastal living. I guess that better matches my paradigm for preservation of the lighthouse keeper's quarters."

He tossed the fork onto the empty plate. "Still, so many more people will see and enjoy the structure in Beaufort. Did you know my hometown has been voted America's coolest small town? And I can tell you, we regard historic preservation as a matter of keen civic pride."

She noticed a flicker of animation in his expression. "Well, who would have thought historic preservation would put a sparkle in your eyes like that? For a devoted veterinarian, salvaging an antique building seems off the mark."

"A man can enjoy many worthy endeavors. In all honesty, my clinic sits right across the street from the platted historical site. I catch glimpses of that trolley running back and forth from the marina all day. We have a handful of federal-period houses, a jail, an apothecary, the old courthouse, and even a vintage doctor's office."

"Plus an animal doctor across the street," she added in a teasing tone. "I noticed you said *we*, so you must be a supporting member of the historical society."

"Guess they have to claim me since my father served on the Board for twenty years, and his father before him. Neither man gained any pleasure when I turned their long-standing physician's office into my animal clinic, but you can't beat that prime location a block from the waterfront right on Turner Street."

"You have a lot to look forward to once back on the mainland. After I get the keeper's house settled on its new foundation, I'll have to research another project to undertake. That's the nature of my business. I have to go to my clients since they won't come to me."

He rose from the table and stretched his arms over his head. "Yes, most of my clients come to my clinic's door, but this evening, I doubt a certain pony will think twice regarding my whereabouts. We'd better go find Stormy, since the tide has already turned at the inlet. I don't want to fight a raging current as high tide pulses in. Nice shell collection, by the way."

"Call it a perk of beachfront living on Core Banks. I don't want to leave my whelk shells behind, but they sure get heavy to lug around."

"Stash them inside the dining room's built-in bench, and you'll gain automatic transport before the summer ends. Voila, special delivery courtesy of a tugboat and barge."

"Well played, Judd. That plan either makes you a genius or a schemer, but I'll take the idea and run with it since I dearly want those shells. Let me grab a lantern in case Stormy puts us through our paces. Follow me back through the house, and we'll leave out of the back door."

"I'll double check the oven's been turned off. At this point, you don't want to lose your project to negligent fire damage."

"Perish the thought, kind sir. Except for the add-on rear storage room, the entire original house will be making this relocation voyage to the mainland."

He trailed her through the two front rooms and wandered over to check the oven setting in the kitchen. "This would look grand sitting in Beaufort on a manicured plot. We could add some of your American beach grass in a foundation planting for authenticity."

She couldn't stop the faltering smile. "I had sea oats drawn into the planting plan, but you're right. That would be a personal touch to commemorate my involvement, one bearing your silent nod of approval." She located the lantern and posed like the Statue of Liberty.

He hesitated in passing toward the door. "Yes, a silent nod between two island researchers. I would consider it a personal favor if you keep Beaufort within the realm of realistic consideration."

"The national park service has to conduct a series of public hearings to take input from all constituents on the matter of relocation of a registered heritage building, so many voices will speak toward this old frame's future. It's not my decision. I'm merely the delivery girl."

He knocked his knuckles on the weathered door of the rear storage room as they descended the back porch. "Poor discard. You would have made a great visitor's center filled with postcards of the Cape Lookout lighthouse."

She chuckled. "And whelk shells galore. Yes, I just might have to reconsider that option." Choosing to trail her guest by a step, she took inventory of the exile's attributes. A solitary inch taller than her at most, the veterinarian bore a sturdy construction under his tanned exterior. Perhaps with less face-bush and a haircut, he might actually look presentable.

A slight breeze caused a tendril of hair to tickle her neck so she handed him the lantern and took a few seconds to work on a repair. "I don't suppose you have a trick whistle or secret call to lure the swimming steed back into your vicinity, do you?"

"No. Stormy is a wild pony. The park service makes sure the Shackleford herd remains feral. Domestication would likely represent their undoing. For various reasons, I try not to train any of the equines. In fact, Stormy made the crossing earlier under duress, but relented at my insistence. I broke several cardinal rules in coming today, including a few promises to myself. Still, the baked flounder tasted delectable and the company proved more than amazing. Plus, I don't get to enjoy oceanfront views very often."

She hid her warm reaction at his pleasure by heading up the sea ox-eye path that led to the grass planting. Within minutes, they found the pony mere steps from where they had left it. She noticed several cropped clumps of grass, a minor penalty for keeping the crossing companion contained for ready retrieval. "Ta-da. I think Stormy found his happy spot."

"Both a renegade and a traitor." He slid his hand under the halter. In steps, he forced the issue of departure. After nibbling one final mouthful of grass, the pony complied.

She accepted possession of the lantern and strolled along on the opposite side of the swimming steed. As for the doctor, their paths diverged at this juncture, a common theme in her line of work. She wouldn't make some empty comment about meeting again on the mainland to render the pending farewell less truncation. No, life along the coast had a way of tamping down such dreams. Instead, she bore up under duty, though today, business and pleasure had surely mingled. Distracted, she hadn't noticed their arrival on the sound's edge until the pony jerked to a halt.

Judd shirked off the faux tux T-shirt and stuffed it into his gear bag. "We bid you a neighborly adieu, Shaina. Should the current ever pull you in the direction of Shackleford Banks again, you can look up your old pal Stormy and his gang of wandering equines. Thank you for an unforgettable dinner and the extra tart for breakfast." With a pat on his waterproof bag, he ducked the pony's neck, took and kissed her hand, and then waded out into the rippling waters of Core Sound, right out of her life.

She rubbed the pony's flank as it stepped into the water to follow. Paralyzed by a sudden feeling of abandonment, she watched their crossing until the lighthouse flashed to greet the descending twilight. *Wretched impenetrable isolation.* The sooner she could move that keeper's quarters, the better. She turned and retraced her steps to go wash dishes left from a memorable dinner-for-two. Somewhere beyond the glasswort patch, the first tear tracked down her cheek.

Chapter 3

Judd waved the captain closer as the square stern of a work boat drifted to better align with the dilapidated dock on historic Wade's Shore. He'd repacked the specimen jars twice since coming back last night too keyed up to sleep. Somehow, a migrating keeper's quarters had taken front stage in his considerations, a definite sideline from scientific study.

"How's it going over here?" the captain shouted over the diesel engine.

"Wrapping up as expected, Skip. Thanks for arriving on time as the sun is beginning to bake the island this morning."

"Yep. Supposed to climb upward toward ninety-five today." He tossed a bow line and reversed the engine.

Judd wrapped a figure eight around the dock cleat and watched as the line pulled taut. "Definitely a good day for departing. I've got everything stashed for safe transport."

"Ha. Everything but a pony, you mean."

"Right. I have parts, but not a full specimen. Let's leave them to their island freedom until I can get some results and make my recommendations. Can you give me a hand with the tent? That's my biggest piece."

Skip took a nimble step over the gunwale and landed both feet onto the dock. "Well, they said you might be stark-raving mad by the time these two months ended, but you seem none the worse for wear to me."

He paused as they both bent to grab the tent roll. "Still, I've seen some ugly sights out here. How unspeakable to take such a pristine environment and permit it to corrode like this. I spent yesterday administering the tick prevention topical wipe to as many members of the herd as possible. I saved that treatment for last, not wanting to contaminate my samples."

"Lift on two. One, two." The captain grunted but cleared his end from the ground.

Judd backpedaled toward the boat. Skip knew the score out here on Shackleford Banks. Aware of that fact, the head ranger seemed apathetic. Maybe the park service had little vested interest here. He set his jaw as his end of the tent cleared the dock and hovered over the boat.

"Give me a step or two, Pearce. You're about to knock me into the water."

In the interim, the tent doubled its weight. His forearms began to protest, so he squatted to lower the burdensome load onto the stern's deck. "I'm dropping my end."

Skip gave his armful a shove and let it land. "There you go. Gonna be a beast to lift out."

"Wait until you get your hands on those boxes

of specimen jars."

The captain wiped his chin across his shirt sleeve. "Mighty sorry to hear about Atlantica passing away. I've watched him roam these dunes for two decades at least. Guess you had to sample him, too?"

He nodded in response. At least the boat operator felt some measure of sentimentality regarding the plight of Shackleford's ponies. He'd hate for their future to parallel the sea turtles' disappearance, a slow demise. For his research, the null hypothesis denied human interference in the resident equine population's wellness, the stance his sponsor questioned. *Trust your eyes.* He'd seen a majority of the foals born with hoof deformities. That led to a conflicted conclusion, one he would allow the scientific evidence to validate.

"Where are those specimen packs, Judd? Let's get loaded up so the wind will be at our backs, and the rising tide can carry us to the mainland." Skip clapped as if to indicate a simple reacquaintance awaited their return.

Judd glimpsed eastward where the marshy rim of Core Banks lined the horizon and hid the ocean. All things hidden would be made known. The specimen jars held irrefutable proof. *Regrettable business, this research.* Dread weighed his arm as he gestured toward the first box.

~

Though Shaina had ordered a maritime transport expert, the park service's tendency to select the lowest bidder had delivered an amateur barge operator for the task instead. She eyed the blue chalk lines that detailed planes of separation for the historic structure, wishing fewer cut lines were possible. "Are you sure there's not a larger barge available to make the crossing, Reo? We could literally transport the house in two halves if we could use a bigger boat."

The cocky man laughed. When he shook his head, his wavy black hair glistened in the sunlight. "Where are you going to dock this hypothetical monstrosity of a larger barge? New Orleans? The draft of a bigger boat would be too deep for the Morehead City landing. I'd be in trouble clearing the Harkers Island dock, too."

"Still, I'm all about the structural integrity of the house. That's my top priority."

"But that's pie in the sky, sister, when you're making a water crossing. It's more important that the boat fits the dock, not that the house fits the barge. I gave you the square footage of the barge deck, so figure it out. The demolition crew can open more seams. We'll provide an extra crossing, if needed. Then the carpenters on the mainland can stitch the old place back together with a few extra nails, a real Humpty Dumpty mending job." He folded his arms, looking like a certified dunce who'd just skipped to the front of the class.

"That leaves me with two planes of cleavage for three identical sections. I reserve the right to keep the front section of the keeper's quarters undivided. That's what the public will view the most, so I intend to preserve both its structural and aesthetic integrity. I refuse to compromise on that point." She buried her heels in the sand.

Reo walked up one side of the structure and then the other. After his feeble inspection, he threw his arms over his head. "Okay, fine. That's going to cost an extra trip over here and back. If the federal people ask any questions, I'm blaming you directly for the cost overrun."

She put her hands on her hips. "You underbid the work just to win the contract. The keeper's quarters didn't shrink one square foot. You undercalculated to keep the cost estimate low. I think we can split the extra expense and consider that a lesson learned."

"Wrong. It costs me more fuel to get back over here. All it will cost you is more time."

A burning sensation began to sour her stomach. She hadn't thought in terms of fuel costs for the extra trip. Such oversight made her the amateur operator. "That sounds like middle ground then. I'll cover the extra fuel costs, but you may have to incur other related costs, like your time as tugboat captain."

He gave her a wise-guy smile. "My time investment depends on which port-o-call is selected for your salt-air shack. My money is riding on Morehead City. They seem to be the most vocal about gaining the historic landmark."

She saw right through his rationale. "You make the most money off the Morehead City run since you gave a sliding quote based on the distance hauled. Harkers Island has a loyal contingency. And I've learned that Beaufort is committed to pursuing possession for its historic site on Turner Street. Maybe it would go well with the maritime museum there. Who knows?"

He gave the notion a dismissive laugh. "I plan on being at the public hearing next Thursday since my uncle got appointed primary speaker for the Harkers Island fan club."

"Great. I'll see you next week then. I think we're done for today. I'll give you an update after the demolition crew comments on the proposed separation lines. Have a nice trip back to the mainland." She dusted some imaginary sand from her hands, hoping to be shed of him.

"Oh, I'm never in any hurry to leave Core Banks. I brought a spare fishing rod over in my skiff so I can wet a line down on cape pointe. Want to come sit a spell with me and watch the surf roll in?" He flexed a few muscles in his right arm as if dangling a masculine lure.

Like his sliding proposal, the guy seemed too shifty. "No, thanks. I have some photo-documentation to finish before the demo guys give me input. By all means, go enjoy your alone time with the ocean."

"I won't be alone…once I get that first fish on the hook. I plan to catch dinner for half the Tillett clan before I head back to Harkers Island. Wander on out if you get caught up." He shot her a sly wink and took a few steps back.

"See you next week at the public hearing, Reo." She turned and headed for the rear stoop, studying the angle of the sun on the western flank of the keeper's house. Nothing on cape pointe interested her anyway. She glanced beyond the lighthouse toward Shackleford Banks. *Wonder how the ponies are?*

A smile tugged at her cheek at the remembrance of Judd Pearce kissing her hand, his overgrown whiskers tickling her knuckles with the gallant gesture. Yes, she'd go paddleboarding later, her weak attempt to close the gap between her and the good doctor. A fickle island resident, she'd forgotten to check the tide charts this morning. Whether rise or fall, the ocean remained a zone of prohibition. Today she could add cape pointe to that exclusion, a veritable land mine of the fisherman kind.

Chapter 4

Judd hadn't missed the disinfectant smell of the animal clinic one bit. He studied the appointment calendar and could tell business would be nonstop all day. He'd wear that press as his reward for being sidelined on research duty for the past two months.

His sister slapped a pencil on the counter. "Oh, my goodness. You haven't heard a single word I've been saying, Judd. Did you go deaf out on Shackleford Banks?"

"Sorry, Jenna. I've got a lot on my mind. Plus, I stayed up way too late cataloguing the specimen jars before shipping them out this morning for chemical analysis. At least the collection phase of the project is out of my hands."

"I said I would take the ear mite cleaning appointment at one for you. I also have two grooming sessions this afternoon. Just remember, when school gets out at three-fifteen, I'm a goner. Mom promised to bring lunch by, so that's one less thing we have to cover."

He pressed his palms against the counter. "Can you help me brainstorm on something else for a minute? It has to do with that lighthouse keeper's quarters relocating from Cape Lookout later this summer. Dad's on the committee for the historical society to make the presentation for Beaufort as a relocation site."

She reclaimed the pencil. "So? What's your angle?"

He blew out a breath which pulled his clean-shaven cheeks tight. "Might as well get this said up front. I met somebody interesting while out on Shackleford. She's the preservationist overseeing the relocation project. When Shaina struggled on her SUP crossing the inlet, I swam out and gave her a hand."

"Go ahead and knock me over with a feather." She exaggerated a bug-eyed stare. "My little brother has taken notice of something that has two legs—not four? It's about time."

The door jingled open with the first client of the day, a droopy Shar-Pei in the arms of the mayor's wife. Judd hesitated to change the topic of conversation, so he viewed the local busybody as a possible ally. "What do you think, Mrs. Wallace? When the lighthouse keeper's quarters are relocated from Cape Lookout in August, do you think that barge should head for Beaufort as its final resting place? I defer to your depthless maritime wisdom."

"Thank you, Dr. Pearce." She stepped closer and deposited her pet on the front counter. "Yes, we want that old relic. The first time I laid eyes on that structure during a girl scout outing to Core Banks years ago, I thought the workmanship was sublime. Wish I could say the same for my little Kismet.

He's simply not his usual vigorous self."

Judd scooped up the pet with a quick wink to Jenna. "Let's have a closer look at what might be occluding this little ray of sunshine." He headed for the first examination room to get the check-up underway, though regret for the return to routine dug at his midsection. Those days on Shackleford represented a shift in his tempo, a boundless freedom he loathed to relinquish. *Wanderlust like a pony running the dunes.* Unfocused, he reached for a swab after placing the animal on the exam table. He hesitated, oblivious as to which end of the critter to probe.

~

Shaina wanted the huge horse conch, but knew her load had already reached capacity. The old straw bag strained from the weight of six newly-deposited whelk shells. After drying on her front porch, she would drop them into the dining room bench and let them await transport out of sight and out of mind. Once she rounded cape pointe, the pounding surf lessened in intensity.

Vowing to make a complete loop by the old war bunker before heading to the lighthouse complex, she scanned the aqueous horizon to look for pleasure boats that might be venturing out to sea early in the week. With the first public hearing scheduled for Thursday night, her free time would soon be crimped. A sand bar had welded to the shore ahead, forming a classic ridge and runnel system which trapped a narrow pool of water inside a spit of sand. "Give and take, little shoreline. It's what you've done for centuries, so don't stop now."

As if cued by the sound of her voice, something dark startled beyond the dune line.

She froze and let an incoming wave wash around her ankles. There stood Judd's equine escort, knee deep in Ammophila and looking antsy. Ears pinned back, the pony regarded her without blinking.

"Hey there, sweet Stormy. Aren't you the clever sport to return for better nourishment?" She eased her phone from her back pocket and snapped a picture to document the vagrant. Sensing the need to surrender the cape to the timid pony, she took a few steps back. "Come anytime you want, Stormy boy. I know Dr. Pearce would approve." She lugged the straw bag along, vowing not to collect another shell unless she spotted an unblemished scotch bonnet between here and the front porch. *Small miracle.*

~

Judd held his forehead in his palms while his half-cocked idea for the Beaufort presentation sank like an ironclad vessel from the Civil War. He needed an invincible plan to land that relocation, but lacked the creativity to pull off a victory.

"Your re-enactment idea turns our pitch into a vaudeville act, son. Let's think of something better." His father balled up the wrapper from his sandwich and tossed it toward the chief cook and picnic packer. "Part of that suggestion does hit home with me. I like the idea of using the old courthouse as our meeting site instead of the public library. That way, we're right on the grounds where the relocation would transpire."

"Plus, we'll have the historic park decorated for the Independence Day celebration," Jenna added. "That might make a favorable impression on the decision committee."

His mother collected the other sandwich wrappers. "Jenna's right. We should maximize our advantage of having July third as our hearing date, for sure. Plus we could invite committee members to stay and be our guests for the Fourth of July parade and fireworks, too. That seems like the neighborly thing to do. Come on, Alan. Think of something better for our pitch."

Judd exchanged glances with his father. Certain he'd like to invite a particular member of the committee to stay for the holiday weekend, he'd hoped to make that personal invitation on the sly. Maybe Jenna had already let that secret scamper out of the bag.

Alan cleared his throat. "Okay, Gracie. We'll extend the invitation and put up any takers in the apartment over our garage. No big deal. As for the presentation on behalf of Beaufort, we're still at square one."

Jenna stood beside the break room table. "I keep having this vision in my head. We're walking past the plot selected for the relocation site on our way to the courthouse and there's a big picture of the lighthouse keeper's quarters showing what the structure would look like standing there. The image is on a giant canvas or something similar to a banner, except almost full scale. Could we possibly rig something on a grand scale like that?"

Judd stood with her, his pulse elevating. "Yes,

seeing leads to believing. We can help the committee visualize the marrying up of the keeper's quarters with our historic park by going ahead and putting a facsimile of it right in place. Great idea, Jenna. You get an A-plus on this history project."

Gracie lifted the picnic hamper and headed out front. "Goodbye, genius children."

Shoulder to shoulder, the probing stare of his father returned. "I'll research the cost of the canvas. You get us an image of the building." With an affirming pat, he exited behind his wife.

Jenna glanced up from wiping crumbs off the table. "How about it? Can you get that image in fairly short order?"

"I don't know. Guess it wouldn't do to lift the black and white image off the public hearing announcement, would it?"

She shook her head. "Look around, Judd. The real world happens in vivid colors—magenta, chartreuse, burnt umber. Read a pack of crayons, for crying out loud. I gotta get the grooming station set up for the two o'clock appointment. See you out in animal land."

He began to wash his hands at the sink, lost in thought as to how to obtain a living color image of the lighthouse keeper's quarters. Sure, he'd dined there not a week ago, but his phone had been dead for over a month so he lacked a camera—a choice he'd made to save on powering up the field generator needlessly. He sighed and dried his hands.

On his way to check the first afternoon appointment, his phone pinged from his pocket. Diverting to the closest exam room, he retrieved the device and checked for a text. A number he didn't recognize came up, labeled New Bern. After clicking to receive the text, he stood staring at Stormy in his nirvana patch of beach grass. Drudgery unhinged its hold and his mood shifted. The pony looked good, almost uncontaminated even. Another ping followed.

Caught him finding his way back to Lookout today. Something to be said for that kind of horse sense! See you in Beaufort on July third.

His thumbs started the return communication before he could finish his thought. *Shaina, big favor to ask. Can you snap the front view of your keeper's quarters and send to me? Creating our presentation and my sister needs a color pic to work from. Many thanks.* He overheard Jenna greeting the next client out front and knew he couldn't hover for a reply. Instead, he struck the send button and resumed his livelihood as a satisfied veterinarian, at least in appearance.

~

Shaina closed her notebook as the first public hearing adjourned. Six citizens from Harkers Island sat in attendance, but only one had spoken. Several of the women served on a refreshment committee, likely their normal level of participation. Even when encouraged to take the microphone, no one else cared enough to register a comment for the record. *What a debacle of first magnitude.* Nora Salter retreated to the back looking pale, but Gibbs hadn't shown up.

Skip Reeder, the head of the park service contingency, stood to his feet. "Well, Mr. Tillett.

We appreciate your presentation tonight. We recognize that Harkers Island and Core Banks share strong ties and a mutual history. Still, our committee needs more than wistful recollections to help us make our final decision. We need a solid relocation plan complete with a designated site for the building. All that came detailed on the public hearing announcement you received. If no one else will give input, I move to conclude this hearing."

Ned Tillett stood and stepped back to the microphone. "Skip, I can't help that our hearing date conflicted with the start-up of a fishing tournament down on Bogue Sound. Half our men are down there trying to win the prize money. We're fishermen, born and bred. That's how we view every day—as another chance to catch a fish."

Skip crinkled the ironed crease in his uniform's sleeve to scratch his head, a subtle stall tactic. "Preservation takes foresight, Mr. Tillett. The man who learns to plan ahead has one eye on the future. Thank you all for coming out tonight. This public hearing is hereby adjourned."

Shaina packed her portfolio without any sense of satisfaction for reaching this juncture. Harkers Island just won a black eye for lack of preparedness, at least in her estimation. If she read Skip Reeder's tone right, they hadn't won him over, either. In one week, Beaufort would have to up the ante. She'd done her part, sending Judd the stamp-sized image that held an ounce of hope for increased enthusiasm. After nodding to Skip, she headed out for the mosquito-infested parking lot to drive back to New Bern.

A rustling motion from the tailgate of a pickup truck startled her. Under poor lighting, she could see a man approach her as other participants got into their cars. Not sure whether to be threatened in such a laid-back setting, she swallowed and walked to her vehicle, alert and wary.

"So that's what you're driving," the man said with a slur in his tone.

She patted the older model Jeep Cherokee while illuminating his face with her key fob. *Not Reo trouble again.* "Yes, she sure gets me around. I had to put a rescued sea turtle in the back hatch once. That made for a quick trip to the marine resource center."

"Afraid my gramps would have eaten that thing instead. He claimed *turkle meat* tastes mighty good."

She backpedaled as his breath smelled like a brewery. "Sorry you missed the public hearing, Reo. Your uncle mentioned the village men had gone down to a fishing tournament."

"Yeah, we ripped our net hauling in so many fish. I'll go back in the morning."

She opened the car door, intent on leaving. "Listen, I've got a long drive ahead of me so I need to get going. I'll be in touch once the selection committee has made a decision. August first remains our target date for transport, so plan to be available."

"I'm always available for you, Shaina. Call me anytime."

When he leaned closer with what resembled romantic intentions, she dropped into the driver's seat and slammed the door. The automatic door locks took care of the rest of his threat. She growled in protest and fired up the ignition. After backing out in haste, she pulled onto the highway which quickly transitioned into the bridge off the island.

No sooner had her wheels crossed the bridge's elevated planking than her phone rang inside her purse. Still dumbfounded by the islanders' failure to make a convincing presentation, she eased onto the shoulder and took the call. "Hello?"

"Hey, Shaina. Judd Pearce here. I thought your public hearing might have ended by now, so I wanted to switch your mindset to a more favorable option, beautiful Beaufort, North Carolina. Hope you have a minute to talk."

"Sure. We just adjourned, but the meeting lacked one key component—advocacy. Only one person spoke, Reo's uncle, Ned Tillett, who turned out to be fairly unconvincing. In fact, I think Skip Reeder took offense at their lack of vision for the restoration project."

"Hey, thanks for that picture you sent me. That will be the star of our presentation, but I don't want to give away too much ahead of time. I called to invite you to stay over in Beaufort to enjoy our Independence Day celebration. The committee chairman, my dad, is offering the garage apartment if anyone on the selection committee wants to stay in town and participate."

"Wow, that's super nice of you guys."

"I wanted to make my invitation more personal. I'd like to show you around town, Shaina, take you to the parade along the waterfront, and tour you through the historical park. You can meet my family and see the animal clinic, too. Will you consider my invitation to celebrate America Beaufort-style?"

An empty black road stared back at her. "You know, Judd, that sounds pretty special. Ask Mr. Chairman to reserve that garage guest room for me. Thanks for the invite, but I need to get rolling." She ended the call and mashed the accelerator, trying to figure out what to aim for ahead and what to leave behind. The wax myrtles failed to wave as she headed ever inland.

Chapter 5

Though his father had made the suggestion, Judd's restless heart had cast the deciding vote for a Saturday excursion to Core Banks. Even for a ten o'clock departure, the ferry landing cooked under the late June sun. He parked under the shade of a twisted live oak and grabbed the cooler from the floorboard. Shouldering into the backpack, he triggered the lock, zipped the key fob away for safekeeping, and headed for the dock.

Other day-trippers milled about the parking lot, seeming restless to break away from the mainland. The ferry rode the dock tethered by heavy lines. An old pickup truck rolled by and deposited the boat captain at the ticket depot.

He glanced at the exiting truck, surprised to recognize the driver. "Hey there, Nora. How's it going?"

She gave a quick glance in the rearview mirror, her expression taut. "Sorry Gibbs is running late. Mosquitoes sure have been bad lately. Not much we can do about that."

"My plan is to outrun the pests over on Lookout today."

A glimmer of a smile appeared on her age-wrinkled face. "That's the lure, ain't it? Too hard to stay away from the ocean and all that sand. You go on over and have a good time."

"Thanks. Hope you have a good day, too." A foghorn sounded from the waterfront, drawing him away. He waved and trotted for the dock, the cooler growing heavier by the minute. Maybe he'd overloaded the ice, but figured Shaina could use the leftovers. He joined the line for tickets, his last commitment before making the crossing. *No turning back.*

The captain gestured at the sign. "That'll be seven-fifty, please."

He handed over a ten and waited for change. "Say, would you know when low tide happens at Barden's Inlet today?"

"Two fifty in change and two-thirty for low tide, give or take ten minutes. Light winds today, so that won't hold up the slack tide none." He nodded sideways in dismissal.

Judd pocketed the money and took a spot in line to board the ferry. Core Sound mirrored the sky, determined to keep the barrier islands out of reach for those not owning boats. Why did he have to drift to the continent's rim so often? The answer might be held in the shadow of the lighthouse today, a truth he needed to explore further.

Gibbs Salter strode past and unclipped the cordon rope to open the passenger ferry for boarding. A family of five scampered aboard and headed toward the bow to claim their seats. The captain checked his watch and glanced toward the parking lot.

He surrendered his ticket and crossed for the starboard railing where a faded blue bench awaited occupancy. A dark bird flushed from the adjoining marsh, and he caught a glimpse of the moorhen before it sheltered in taller grass. Moments later, the ferry's diesel engines fired up and the deck quivered to life. Once the stern line broke free, the excursion took on momentum.

The captain had just turned the bow's tip south when a blaring horn sounded from the parking lot. Seeming aggravated, he muttered something negative under his breath and reversed the engines. The ferry backed toward the dock, making a hard scrape when the two reacquainted.

A late female passenger ran down the dock, waving her thanks to the boat operator.

Thinking to help out, Judd sprang to his feet to unclip the restraining line and let her board. One glance at her tanned legs gave him more motivation to lend a hand. *Almost missed her by half a minute.* Pulling the line back, he bowed and gestured for her to enter. "Welcome, Shaina. Glad you could make it." He slid the sunglasses down his nose to aid her recognition.

Her expression froze a split second, and then the boat lurched forward as if to make up time. She clasped his arm for support and widened her stance. "Oh, wow. Of all the folks I didn't expect over on Lookout today."

"Here, join me by the red cooler." He led her to the bench, unable to suppress his delight. "What? No receptivity for an off-duty veterinarian who needs to see the ocean?"

She squeezed her eyes closed. "Something told me to come back today. I typically return on Sunday afternoons, but New Bern grew hostile with my mother's insistence that I find my next job. Government bids typically come out the first of the month, so I'll have to wait for some promising opportunity to find me later."

"And everyone knows the beach never harbors any hostility." He peered over his glasses to give her an impish look. "At least not in fair weather. By the way, our good captain says that the tide will be low at the inlet by two-thirty. Do you think I could make reservations for a lesson on your SUP? I brought us lunch, if that might help persuade you."

She tightened the tie on her straw hat as the ferry gained momentum. "Are you attempting to go see Stormy? Is that what this trip is about?"

"Not at all. Presumptuous as it might seem, I hoped to enjoy the leisure company of the resident relic architect. It never crossed my mind you might be off the island."

She let the duffel bag slip off her shoulder. "Well, in that case, I could show you the new division lines for the keeper's quarters. I couldn't be happier to report that we located a larger barge that will allow the building's relocation in two trips, not three. We'll move the house's rear half first, so the installation can transpire back to front. How's that for ultimate efficiency?"

He leaned closer until the brim of his ball cap doffed the rim of her hat. "Breakthroughs look amazing on you, Miss Gillespie. After your tour, I'll claim any spare time you have and be most grateful for the unparalleled company. I'm on Lookout until the dune buggy blows its horn for the final departure."

She smoothed a hand over her bare shoulder. "Let's make it a day to remember, Judd. I still need to pinch myself that you're actually here. With the haircut and shave, I almost didn't recognize you. Not too sure I'll miss that throwback hippie look, to be honest."

He laughed at her interpretation of his negligence while living on Shackleford Banks. "No, those research days are behind me now. Only blue skies ahead."

"And blue ocean. Hope you don't mind, but I need to comb the shore for seashells. My days living on the beachfront are numbered, so I have to make each one count." She placed her hand over his on the bench and gave it a light pat.

Enthralled to have Shaina so close, he wove his fingers through hers and studied the low-slung horizon stretching before them. The slender bar of sand guarding the sound held more than seashells. How much more, he would try to discover with a bit of close-held interest.

"What's in the cooler?"

"The lunch I packed for us—with extra ice—just in case."

"Wow. You really know how to tempt a girl. Want to eat on the front porch again?"

"Or at the top of the lighthouse, whichever you prefer."

She answered with a toying smile. "I do have

the key."

The ferry banked east toward Core Banks, making him look beyond her to the island. A returning sense of freedom overwhelmed him. As the ferry slowed, the sultry salt air thickened the breeze. "Let's stash the cooler in the shade of the front porch and go shelling. Then we'll grab lunch in plenty of time to make the two-thirty paddleboard lesson." When her little smile reappeared, he had all the permission he needed to enjoy his Saturday off the mainland.

~

Shaina attributed Judd's ease of movement to his compact stature since he had taken right to the paddleboard without any difficulty. "Maybe shift back half a step to better center your weight." She watched him maneuver and then head back out to sea again with a powerful stroke. "Good work, but your arms are going to be sore tonight."

He raised the paddle over his head and shook it, as if putting his domination on display.

She knelt along the sound's edge and dug a finger into the marsh mud to hunt for occupants. Maybe she could excavate an oyster drill with any luck. When she glanced up, Judd approached in high gear. She stood and washed the grit from her knees. "Hey, what's up?"

"The ponies just took the spit over on Shackleford. Come watch them with me. Can this thing hold both of us?"

"I've seen tandem boarding before, but never tried it. We only have one paddle."

"Then you'll be my guest." He beckoned to her

from the shallows.

Since she'd selected the maker's most stable model, she now had to count on eleven feet of flotation to hold them both above Core Sound. Better than roasting back on the shore, she waded out for the pony excursion. "Maybe only go halfway, as the tide has likely shifted by now. When currents go ripping through the inlet, it always spells trouble for me."

He gripped her hand and pulled her closer. "Nah, don't forget that's how we met. You stand up front and leave me room to paddle."

She placed one knee on the board and shifted the other on with a gradual nudge. As she attempted to stand, his arm wrapped her waist and steadied her frame. In an act of trust, she straightened her bent knees to stand on the wobbly board.

Judd reached for his cap and turned the brim backwards. "Here, slip your feet between mine so our weight merges. A knuckle brushed against her shoulder blade. "Wow, your back is hot." He lifted the paddle and let water trickle onto her overheated skin.

"Okay, let's take this tandem ride slow. The ponies will wait for us—or we'll catch them another day." She leaned back and felt him take the first paddle stroke, a muscular venture. Riding as a twosome birthed a heady attraction as they made progress across the inlet. Any separation led to an immediate imbalance, so she stayed close. The rhythm of his paddling soon overrode her worry of capsizing the burdened vessel.

Judd rubbed his nose on her ear. "I like this duo

SUP mode better than solo riding. It makes for more of a balancing game, for sure."

She let magnetic attraction hold her in place. "Oh, and I thought proximity made it superior, good doctor. Funny you've called it a balancing game. Should I move forward half a step, you might call it an imbalanced game." She looked over her shoulder and misjudged his immediate position. He stood closer than close, a mesmerizing happenstance.

A wet thumb slipped across her jawline as if to hold her in place. "Imbalance is the better word." He matched her position, touched his sun-baked lips to hers, and held the weightless embrace as the paddling rhythm halted.

A wobble cut into the kiss. Shana shifted one foot forward and tried to stabilize the SUP. Before she knew it, she was halfway doing the splits. When the imbalance grew too much to overcome, she fell off the right side straight into the sound. Once she'd surfaced, she discovered Judd had jumped in after her.

"Are you okay?" He gave her an intense stare. "Should I check for head trauma again?"

She caught his cap as it tried to float away on the incoming current. "No head trauma this time, but is it too late to request the horse liniment?"

He laughed and pulled her into his arms. "You're right to ask for more treatment. I think I have just what the doctor ordered." He took the cap from her, put it on backwards, and leaned in to deliver his cure.

Shaina held onto the board as the current flowed like time streaming by while Judd's second kiss lingered, a refreshing time-out from the pressing forces of nature. She touched the stubble along his sideburns, awash in the sensation. *Time and tide wait for no man.* But maybe a fallen mermaid could get a reprieve, given the right crossing pattern.

Chapter 6

At Skip's lead, Shaina entered the conference room of the local park service office. Not too humored at having a Harkers Island detour, her demolition crew arrived tomorrow to detach the back porch from the keeper's quarters. She restrained her objections and took a far side seat in deference to Skip's authority. The captain's chair belonged to him as chairman of the site selection committee. The lawyer from New Bern remained absent, so they lacked a quorum.

A few subdued whispers in the hall led to an incoming parade of Harkers Island women. From all appearances, they resembled the same contingency that had attended the public hearing not two weeks ago. They selected seats on the closer side of the conference table and sat down.

Skip cleared his throat. "Since this is an informal gathering, I'll dispense with meeting protocol. Still, I felt it important to take input today, so I've called Shaina Gillespie to join us. Because of the short lead time, the remainder of the selection committee won't be attending. I'll ask each speaker to state her name so we can record it with your comments. Mrs. Salter, since you contacted me to request this meeting, I'll ask you to go first."

Shaina tried to read the expressions of the women, a silent majority that held the island's social connections together, albeit typically from the back row. A heavy-set woman elbowed the woman on the end and gave a stern nod. Beside her, a thin woman who wore her hair in a braid sniffed and drew out a tissue from her purse to dab her nose.

The woman seated on the end rose to her feet. "Thank you, Mr. Reeder. I'm Nora Salter, a lifelong resident of Harkers Island. We appreciate this opportunity to express our interest in inheriting the lighthouse keeper's quarters from Cape Lookout. In general consensus, we felt our husbands botched the first attempt to relay our affection for gaining the old building at the public hearing. In retrospect, we should have spoken up before today. I regret that silence. Sometimes a person gets so used to playing second fiddle to the point where they feel like they don't have a say anymore. Still, we're true Americans here on the island, and each of us possesses the constitutional right to express our opinions. Today at this meeting, we plan to do just that."

Shaina tried to record Nora's comments as best she could. The woman's late-arriving moxie was to be applauded. For an instant, Judd flashed to mind. Would he be the silencing type like these women's domineering husbands? Her shoulders shook with an involuntary quiver to cast the notion aside.

"Ned Tillett accepted the job as speaker," Nora

continued. "In truth, he experienced a spell of vertigo from an ear infection so the doctor ordered him off his boat for three weeks. That meant he couldn't fish the tournament. All the specifics we'd discussed earlier dropped by the wayside when Ned went off script into a bunch of generalities that sounded more like a pep talk. Today, we'll fill in some of those details regarding what it would look like to harbor the keeper's house on Harkers Island. If these comments could be amended to our presentation, we would be beholden to the selection committee." She dropped back into her seat, her neck reddened from the confession.

The heavy-set woman stood next. "I'm Jean Lane. Regarding location, we've reserved an adequate plot beside the church cemetery for the keeper's house. The land is low there, we recognize that, but it's right by the highway so we can show off our historic treasure."

The thin woman stood beside her. "My name is Raye Poole. About the foundation, we'll use concrete blocks cemented together and leave an access door in the rear, in case anybody has to crawl under there for maintenance. We'll have to take up a collection to pay for those materials, but I think the churches in town might help us out." She shrugged and sat down, tugging at the arm of her acquaintance to do the same.

With a great deal of hesitation, the last woman stood. "I'm June Tillett, Ned's wife. Part of what my husband said contains the central truth to our bid for the keeper's house. One can hardly mention Harkers Island without Core Banks creeping into the conversation. It makes total sense for us to inherit the historic building being brought off Cape Lookout. The wax myrtles and yaupon will form such a scenic backdrop for the house, in a few years it will look like an original setting. Thanks for letting us speak our piece today. We really want that old building."

Nora Salter rose again. "There's been some talk of putting together a walking tour of historic structures along the main roads of our community. We'd add the original ferry dock and the settlers' well to that tour docket, but the sweetheart of the collection would be the keeper's house, standing in all its grandeur. We'll end on that note, so you know our hopes and dreams of the future rest on your decision to bring the building here. Thank you for hearing us out. That's all we have to present."

As if cued, the women rose from their seats, locked elbows, and paraded out of the room.

Shaina recorded the last comments and then tossed her pen onto the legal pad. After blowing out a pent-up breath, she ventured a glance at Skip. The chairman seemed deep in thought. "I believe we may have just witnessed a mutiny of sorts—a rebellion of mild-mannered women."

Skip half-snorted a chuckle. "We'll include their comments as a postscript to the public hearing records and distribute them to committee members. While I think their hearts are in the right place, the lack of support by the Harkers Island men may lead to pesky negligence for the structure in the long run. Let's hold off deciding and see what the people of Beaufort can offer."

She nodded and packed up her papers. She had a stamp-sized investment in that presentation. Those two kisses would go without mention. *Keep it fair.* If only she could.

Chapter 7

Judd sat in the second row behind the historical society members. He held an empty seat for Jenna as the old courthouse filled to the brim with avid supporters. Proud that his community had rallied behind the project, he scanned the vaulted room and counted two dozen clients in the mix. His apprehension jumbled multiple conversations close by until the space filled with an indistinguishable buzz.

Jenna stepped across the couple seated by the aisle. "So sorry I'm late. Had some last-minute rigging to do. I hope everything comes off as planned."

"Is the canvas ready for the unveiling?"

"You bet. The lighting add-on put me through some extra paces, but we're good to go."

He smiled at her in collusion. "I hope the townspeople remember tonight's public hearing fondly years from now when they walk by the keeper's quarters nestled in downtown Beaufort."

She sat down and smoothed out her skirt. "Look who's counting their chickens."

"You can't keep a good Pearce down."

His father turned around from the front row and gave them a sly wink. The historical society appeared well-prepared for the night's challenge. An equal pairing of men and women, the venerable committee recognized the high stakes, yet faced the hearing undaunted.

The selection committee entourage took the platform in a show of collective authority. Several of the members dressed in park service uniforms. Shana wore a salmon-colored blouse that folded into a ruffle down the middle over a tailored navy skirt.

Jenna jabbed an elbow into his shoulder. "Holy cow, Judd. Is that Shaina Gillespie?"

His throat went dry. "Yep. That's Shaina, my paddleboard instructor."

"Will wonders never cease? She's a dark-haired beauty, for sure. You've been pretty mum about her, little brother. I'm going to introduce myself after the unveiling."

"Remember, you're going to meet her tomorrow. We're all having lunch together downtown at Waterfront Park after the parade." He rubbed the sight of her jab and checked the time. An elderly couple filed into their row and occupied the last two seats.

Skip Reeder took the podium. "Thank you all for coming out tonight for the second public hearing regarding the pending placement of the lighthouse keeper's quarters from Cape Lookout. We welcome all relevant comments from the public at large, but have agreed to extend the starting comments to the Beaufort Historical Association members for their presentation at this time." He gestured toward the front row before retaking his seat.

Judd noticed Shaina scanning the crowd from the platform and searched for a way to make his location known. When the line of presenters stalled while taking the stage, he stood and offered his father's best friend a good-luck handshake. For an infinitesimal second, he locked gazes with Shaina and flashed a demure one-fingered wave before sitting back down.

"Subtle move, Judd," Jenna whispered. "Now at least she knows where you are."

"At most she knows." He fired off a rapid wink. Anticipation mounted as the men lined up facing opposite the women on stage.

Mrs. Wallace stepped out first. "In seventeen twenty-three, Beaufort became incorporated from an appointment by North Carolina's eight Lord Proprietors to serve expressly as a port for the unloading of goods, and theretofore became the county seat. In seventeen eighty-two, in our nation's quest for independence, the British invaded Beaufort which resulted in the schoolhouse burning down upon their departure." She stepped back in line with a nod to her counterpart.

Mayor Wallace glanced around the room. "In eighteen twelve, the first lighthouse over on Cape Lookout began its service. Limited in height, its effectiveness became the bane of seafaring men along the North Carolina coast. In eighteen fifty-nine, the taller lighthouse was completed, a brick structure of one hundred sixty-three feet with a fixed light that could be seen eighteen miles out to sea."

The next woman, a teller at the main bank, stepped out for duty. "By eighteen sixty-one, North Carolina joined the Confederate States of America. All lighthouse lenses were ordered removed by the Confederate government and placed into storage until after the war. The Beaufort Harbor Guard was placed in charge of Fort Macon. Within a year, Beaufort and Morehead City were captured by Union troops after a brief skirmish at Fort Macon." She shook her head and rejoined the line.

The grocery store owner took his turn with civic pride shining in his eyes. "A daring escapade occurred in eighteen sixty-four when Confederate troops under the command of L.C. Harland snuck through Union lines and approached Cape Lookout lighthouse with destruction as their aim. Partly scuttled, only the oil supply house and some iron stairs up the lighthouse were damaged."

The grocer's wife stepped out with a sweet smile. "During the War Between the States, Union Town became established along the north edge of Beaufort as a refugee camp for freedmen and former slaves. Everybody had a place to call home in Beaufort, our welcoming community."

His father's friend, an insurance salesman, had duty next. "The year was eighteen seventy-three, and a picture postcard-worthy addition came to the Cape Lookout lighthouse—a paint job that included diagonal black-and-white diamonds that have become its trademark look standing out in the sand dunes. That same year, the new keeper's quarters were built to house the lighthouse keeper, two assistants, and their families. Iconic in structural form, these boxy two-story houses with sweeping front porches became an indelible part of scenic Cape Lookout."

As the insurance man stepped back in line, a lump formed in Judd's throat. History meant something dear to him. If by some remote chance they could gain possession of this legendary residence, he would make sure it would remain preserved for future generations to enjoy. His eyes misted at the possibility.

The librarian shifted into center stage. "In nineteen thirty-three, Duke University built a marine laboratory on Piver's Island near our town of Beaufort. During a severe hurricane that September, Barden's Inlet opened between Core Banks and Shackleford Banks, carving a new dimension to the area's navigation."

Judd's father took the helm. "Also in thirty-three, electric lamps were installed in the Cape Lookout lighthouse, requiring the addition of a generator. By nineteen fifty, the lighthouse became fully automated, putting the resident lighthouse keepers out of a job. Upon their departure, the U.S. Coast Guard assumed occupation of the keeper's quarters, a tour of duty that extended through nineteen eighty-two."

His mother picked up on cue. "Another fabulous happening in the nineteen fifties included the organizing of the Beaufort Historical Association. Among its first activities, according to Grandpa Pearce, were historical tours, antique shows, and— my all-time favorite—pirate invasions. In the same decade, the Hampton Mariner's Museum was started on Turner Street, a few feet from where we sit tonight.

"We hope you've enjoyed our recounting of the entwined history of Beaufort and Cape Lookout. Furthermore, we hope this shines a spotlight on our commitment to historical preservation. Next, we have a different kind of spotlight to shine, so we invite everyone to join us on the grounds just south of the courthouse building, or to the left, as my husband insists. Please meet us outside for the concluding portion of our presentation. Thank you."

As the historical association members filed down the aisle, Skip collected the selection committee members to follow their lead. Judd stood, trying to track Shaina as she came down from the platform into the crowd.

Jenna pushed her shoulder into his. "C'mon, starry eyes. You've got to help me run the lighting around the foundation."

"Right. A non-speaking role to keep my conflict of interest to a minimum."

"Oh, you've got conflict brewing, brother. Shaina stared at you practically the entire time. Let Dad run his plan to completion, and then you can show her to the garage apartment."

"After we stroll along the waterfront, you mean."

She plugged two fingers in her ears. "Fa-la-la-la-lo. Details I don't want to know."

He laughed as she became poetry in motion, darting through the side door. He followed, confident this next unveiling would land with dramatic impact. Once in place along the rear of the proposed foundation frame-out, he married the extension cord to the outlet and illuminated the rope light around the relocation site's perimeter. Several members of the crowd made pleasurable exclamations as if viewing fireworks.

Jenna gave the signal and then tugged the rope to let the canvas unfurl. As the roll gained momentum to meet the ground below, several spectators began to applaud. The staccato flash of cameras came next, as several townspeople recorded the moment to become part of their history-in-the-making.

Judd maneuvered around the perimeter to watch the closing presentation. Under subdued lighting, the image of the keeper's quarters appeared surreal. A spotlight joined the ensemble, focused on the structure's front door.

His father stepped into the light beam and squinted. "On behalf of the Beaufort Historical Association, I hereby pledge a dedicated sum of forty-five hundred dollars annually for the general maintenance and upkeep of the lighthouse keeper's quarters, including any subsequent upgrades to improve electrical installation and/or climate control to thwart damaging influences like humidity and variations in temperature.

"In closing, the historical association would like to offer one further concession as the proverbial cherry on top of our solicitation to receive the keeper's quarters. After extensive consideration, we hereby propose to hire a full-time director for the historical park here on Turner Street, to oversee details of preservation as well as run our nonprofit association. Please consider our bid to merge these two histories into one beautiful park. On behalf of countless folks who would get to admire this coastal treasure, we would appreciate your full consideration as a recipient site for the lighthouse keeper's quarters. Thank you very much."

As Skip stepped into the light to shake hands, Judd searched for Shaina in the crowd. Seeing a hand reach up to stroke the canvas, he sidestepped to nip any prank in the bud. Instead, much to his delight, he located his architect friend who stood looking enthralled with the oversized image. "Oh, great. I found you at last."

She turned toward him, her eyes rimmed with tears. "We'd hope to find someone who might revere this old house. What a beautiful presentation, Judd. Remarkable really. This relic seems to fit right in place among the rest of the preserved buildings."

He gave her a quick wink. "See, I tried to tell you, an epic period match-up."

"May I have your attention?" Skip called. "As a matter of due process, I'm required to ask for any further comment from the general public at this time." He held his arms open wide. "Are there any further comments?"

It began in the back along Turner Street like a low rumble. As the chant repeated, the message became more distinguishable. Both syllables of the town's historic name vaulted up in a drumbeat of support.

Judd caught the chant as Jenna joined them.

"Beau-fort, Beau-fort, Beau-fort."

Jenna leaned closer to Shaina. "I'm Judd's sister, Jenna. He really wants to fight for this particular acquisition as a third-generation local historian."

Shaina laughed amid the cheering. "I can see that determination. Congratulations. You guys did a knock-out job tonight."

"Thank you all," Skip shouted. "This public hearing is hereby adjourned."

Judd hooked elbows with Shaina. "Welcome to hospitality central, Pearce family style." A waggle of his brow finished the sentiment. With the official portion of the evening over, the personal part could take wing. Even when the perimeter lighting extinguished, his hopes stayed lit for an evening stroll along the waterfront where time stood still and let a man live.

~

Though a small town, Shaina sensed vibrancy here in picturesque Beaufort. And they certainly took their civic pride to heart here. Memories of costumed townspeople and festive parade floats stirred her reflections of a perfect Independence Day. Nearby, more boats appeared along the waterfront as dusk began to settle. A girlish giddiness overtook her. She glanced westward to discover the last glimmer of sunset on the far horizon.

Judd hastened up from the closest dock. "Mom and Dad are all set for the show with a boatload of eager spectators. Still, they invited us to come aboard, if you'd like."

A compelling need for stability anchored her to the land. "No, I'd prefer to stay on shore, if you don't mind."

"Right. I'm thinking the same thing." He stepped closer. "Let's go find our own spot." Instead of heading for the heart of downtown, he led off in the opposite direction.

She swirled the remainder of a frozen lemonade slushie and followed. Families sat on quilts by the water's edge, the kids careening in every compass direction chasing each other. *What a sweet slice of American pie.*

Judd halted just outside of a white picket fence that guarded a small gazebo. "How does this look?"

"Like private property." She took a sip of her beverage to hide her grin.

"Nah, my uncle lets me drop in anytime I want to watch the boats go by. Come join me."

"Won't the dome roof block our view of the fireworks?"

"I'm not sure, but if it does, we'll lean out over the railing."

Her pulse kicked up a notch. "That sounds risky."

He opened the tiny gate. "Sometimes the risk is worth the reward. Guess I don't have to tell that to a woman who's about to set a historic house afloat on a wing and a prayer."

She passed him at the gate. "Don't forget the rusty heap of a crane loading it onto the sketchy borrowed barge. I need to have unwavering faith since I can't hold my breath that long."

He grabbed her hand and pulled her toward the

sun-faded canvas hammock. "Forget about all of that for now. If we sit down at the same time, you won't end up in my lap."

She lacked enough lemon frost to quell the heat moving up her neck. "Maybe let me go first, then." When he joined her a split second later, her world began to tilt. Soon afterward, the first firework exploded a glittery chrysanthemum in the sky. The gold dust trailed down toward the water's reflective surface and touched about the time Judd's fingers laced into hers. *What a night to remember.* A cannon blast led to a red and blue explosion next, so she tightened her grip.

Chapter 8

Row after row of empty wooden seats stared back at the selection committee, making Shaina wonder where the good citizens of Morehead City had gone since they weren't attending tonight's public hearing. The town manager and his wife claiming the front row had already spoken on behalf of the city's proposal to incorporate the lighthouse keeper's quarters in an urban block south of the library. Their proposal lacked any zeal and held no contingency for upkeep or maintenance. She rechecked her brief notes and sighed.

Skip Reeder made his classic watch-checking gesture. "I need to ask the general public for any further comments at this point. Are there any further comments or questions?" He scanned the room to complete the procedural requirement. A fellow member of the selection committee growled as if to fill the silence. Skip nodded. "Okay then. I hereby adjourn this public hearing for the Morehead City proposed acquisition of the historic Cape Lookout lighthouse keeper's quarters. Thank you both for coming out tonight."

The man rose to his feet. "I have to shut off the

lights once everybody's out the door."

Skip popped his park service cap in place and grabbed his portfolio. In no time, his heels clicked down the tile flooring toward the front exit.

Shaina gave the woman a slight smile as she hurried behind her driver. The public hearing phase now ended with a hollow thud, leaving them with two underplayed proposals to compare against the spirited pursuit of custody by Judd's hometown.

Skip glanced over his shoulder. "Let's detour at Beaufort on our drive back. I've gotta strong urge to view their historical village one more time. This pending relocation might be the easiest decision I've made in my entire career."

"I'm seconding your stopover motion, Mr. Chairman." The salute she gave him brought a chuckle. Beaufort held undeniable charm, for more reasons than one.

~

Judd examined the crestfallen look on his sponsor's face across the clinic's front counter. "The lab results are in and the data confirms our worst suspicion. The herd shows signs of chemical contamination, right down to the last pony tested. Residues found in sampled tissues mainly confirm benzene derivatives, the kind typically associated with EPA Superfund sites. As you suspected, former military sites like our ammo depot tend to be the worst offenders."

Nora leaned into her folded hands until they hid her face. "They've had so much time to address this horrible blemish on the shore. Silence isn't golden. No, in this case silence stinks like a festering sore. I wish the government could have stayed off of Shackleford Banks in the first place." She paused and made a deep sigh. "Are you certain these results are conclusive?"

He held out the summary table for her immediate inspection. "The data clearly shows contamination in the wild ponies and their habitat. It's a cesspool of toxicity over there, and it needs to be rectified."

She fingered the corner of the paper. "Oh, dear. Look at poor Atlantica. He could have glowed in the dark with all this contamination." She squeezed her eyes shut. "My first reaction is deep sadness. My heart hurts over this negligence. Consider all the time that's past since the big war ended. You think the government could have come behind the defense department in the aftermath to sweep up their own mess."

"Ammo dumps are time bombs typically left ticking for future defusing. Still, you would speculate that someone would have pressed the issue, especially since folks from Harkers Island used to keep summer houses over there."

She sat erect and gave him a piercing glare. "I'll never forget the first time Gibbs showed me the contamination site back in nineteen eighty-one. He called it the *war scab*. The men feared it would contaminate the drinking water, which had always been scarce over there."

A mention of the men caused the hair on the back of his neck to stand. "I can hardly fathom why the community leaders didn't confront the park service over this ammo depot site. They had every right to disclose their genuine concerns."

"Maybe they had a bigger battle to wage. Hints that the park service wanted to take over Shackleford Banks ran rampant in those days. The men clawed and scratched to produce every bit of legal evidence possible that they owned the right to use Shackleford. I sat in my kitchen and kept quiet while us common folks got outmaneuvered by the federal government. Within a year, we had to burn our island houses to the ground and quit using Shackleford except for passive day fishing off the shores."

His throat turned to sandpaper. "They claimed it was to protect the wild ponies, at least that's how my father explained the decision to exclude Harkers Islanders out on the Banks."

Her neck reddened as she grabbed for the summary sheet. "Right, to protect the ponies—or to lock them onto a contaminated island where no one might take notice."

"The hoof deformity makes the evidence hard to question. I believe we have a better case now, and you possess scientific proof the animals have assimilated the benzene contaminant. The passage of time works in our favor, at least in that regard."

She stood, taking the results printout with her. "We'll need your expert testimony once we move forward, Dr. Pearce. Can I count on you?"

He bit the inside of his cheeks. How easy would it be to let the tide continue rolling in on those golden shores? The meadow held a war scab, all right, one that needed to heal. "I'm on standby to serve as your expert witness when you bring the lawsuit. I've already staked off the plot where the grass samples originated. I'll write up my methodology and draw some pointed conclusions from these lab results while I'm waiting to hear from you."

She headed for the front door, a woman on a crusade. "Thank you for accepting this research project in the first place, Dr. Pearce. Confrontation is never pretty, but often necessary."

"We have the burden of proof we need, so we'll let this data do the talking for us." He opened the door with a shrug and flipped on the front porch light.

The sponsor stepped into the heated July night. Tears marked her cheeks. "Poor Atlantica. I rode him as a girl…"

"Wild and free."

She sobbed but held her composure. "I guess *careless* won't allow life to stay *carefree*."

The heady sensation of riding Thunder across the dune ridge suddenly swept across his mind. That freedom had to stand for something. "We'll protect the herd, no matter the cost."

She gave him a hollow stare. "We've already paid the cost, Dr. Pearce. Call that a belated silent scream for justice."

"Let the Harkers Island women know they can count on me." When he recalled that Stormy showed the least amount of contamination, a ray of hope broke into the gloomy night. *Never too late to do what's right.* Maybe they could even accomplish a cleanup without getting confrontational. That would be his thin, grass-starved hope going into the legal battle, an odd stance for a veterinarian that tended mild-mannered dogs and cats by direct comparison.

~

Even by streetlight, Shaina recognized the features of Beaufort's waterfront from her personalized Independence Day tour. A sense of belonging wrapped her in familiar comfort. Maybe she could claim a soft spot for the scenic little town aside from Skip's pending decision.

The driver cleared his throat. "What's the name of that street where the historic plaza is located?"

"Look for Turner Street. I think it's the next left." As the car slowed, she strained to find something familiar on the waterfront. Finally, she spotted the lemonade shop. "Yes, the next left is definitely Turner Street. They should have the converted oil lamps still lit until ten o'clock."

He nodded and soon negotiated the turn. "I may pull into a parking spot so my headlights illuminate the proposed relocation plot. I just need to refresh the image in my mind."

Anxious to see whether the oversized banner still remained, she sat erect and strained to see. Hard to miss, a car remained parked right in from of Judd's clinic. As Skip veered in the opposite direction to gain perspective on the historical park, she caught sight of two figures embracing in a hug along the curb. She clamped her eyes closed in numb disbelief. Needing a follow-up look to be sure, she glanced in the side view mirror in time to watch Judd stroll back up the walkway to call it a night. The image knifed her midsection with cloaked betrayal.

"Really," Skip said. "This location is truly fetching. There's a lot to admire here."

Shaina clenched her fist against her lower ribs to gain a steady breath. "Everything's admirable at first glance, Chairman Reeder. Our job is to make an informed decision, so let's take the time to examine all the criteria. Those Harkers Island women deserve fair treatment."

Skip peered into the rearview mirror, looking a touch befuddled.

"We can head back whenever you're ready." The canvas banner of the keeper's quarters waved to her in the night breeze. *Does that hurt like a farewell gesture?* The ride back took forever, even with the convenience of bridges across the low spots.

Chapter 9

Judd stood at the Beaufort waterfront watching the once-in-a lifetime feat transpire offshore. Despite the relocation victory, nothing had gone right in his personal life since the lab results arrived, a real curse of Jonah. Shaina had called in a steamed huff and slammed the door on their personal involvement. Maybe once the legal papers had been served forcing the cleanup, he could confess his secretive research and ask for some measure of forgiveness.

The rusty barge made slow work of turning perpendicular to shore. Twin engines behind the tug insisted on the maneuver with constant churning of water. Barely offset from the bow's rim, half the keeper's quarters sat hunched, an orphan without the lighthouse anchoring it to the dune line. Its clapboard siding seemed drained to a sun-bleached gray, splintered and wind-whipped compared to the new plywood panels nailed across each window.

A lump formed in his throat, the triumph bittersweet. He'd gained the relic, but somehow lost the architect in the process. His father's sage advice last night involved a strained attempt at explanation, but today would offer little opportunity for honest words of contrition. Regret weighed his euphoria while other onlookers shouted cheers of welcome at the barge's approach.

About fifty yards out, the barge's hull scraped bottom, causing the tugboat to rebound off the port piling. Two figures scampered down the tug's tower and ran forward around the wooden structure, scanning the waterline. The man gestured for the captain to reverse direction.

Transfixed at the unfolding drama, Judd missed the small boat pulling up against the bulkhead. When he looked down, he spotted his father at the helm so he closed the distance between them. "What do you make of this, Dad?"

"The tug ran the barge aground," Alan relayed with animated gestures. "The barge's draft must be too deep, laden with the old house like that."

"Should we go for shovels?"

"How would you stand in water fifteen feet deep to shovel, Judd? Use your thinking cap. There must be another way for us to help."

No two ways about it, the barge had to touch the waterfront's bulkhead, or the flatbed truck waiting to haul the house across the last block of its journey would have to suspend itself over the water. *Not happening.* With his pulse elevated, he spotted Shaina standing on the bow. He scanned the historic structure, looking for any possible seam to divide the load.

Running on instinct, he jogged to the municipal dock and headed down its length. His lungs started to burn so he tried to deep breathe. *Shallow, we need to go shallow.*

The tug's engines moaned in a final attempt to shove the vessel to its destination. The effort gained only a precious few feet more in the needed advance. Catcalls from the crowd began to fill the air and confused the situation further.

Judd cupped his hands around his mouth. "Shaina, you've run aground solid. Hold up on the forward momentum until we can get the bow to ride higher in the water."

She nodded and turned to signal the tugboat captain by dragging a finger across her throat. Tanned and svelte, she made her way forward testing ropes as she went. She jerked a shutter loose on the rear-most window as if to dislodge it.

Memories of their dinner date on the front porch flooded through his mind. *What could lighten the load?* He studied the structure in a clearer mindset.

A familiar boat puttered up to the end of the dock, his father waving him down. "Let me go collect the Coast Guard booms left down by the Taylor Creek outlet. If the tug can pull the barge off the sandy bottom, maybe we can get some of these flotation booms beneath the bow."

"Anything's worth a try at this juncture. See if you can get another boat to catch the far end of those booms so you're not dragging the whole caboodle."

With a salute, the veteran seaman pursued the tentative rescue.

When Judd turned his attention to the structure again, he recognized the back side of the house. That would make the kitchen and dining room the primary features on this load. *Time to jettison anything heavy.* Left with no wiggle room, Shaina would simply have to work with him.

Jenna ran down the dock and stopped short, her chest heaving. "I have the girl's rowing team on standby. What can we do?"

"Go ahead. Have them paddle out." He paused to remember the proper orientation. "Stay west of the barge, but have the girls nose their sculls into the barge's flank. We're going to unload some ballast. That's the only way to lighten up to float these shallows."

She looked at him incredulous. "Which side is west?"

"To the right side. Stay to the right. Avoid anyone getting between the barge and this dock at all cost."

Jenna shot him a thumbs-up and reversed to set his plan in motion.

For the first time, he longed to board the vessel and reach the heart of the action. Maybe the heat of rescue would warm up Shaina's cold shoulder treatment. While he commiserated with a bruised ego, he trotted to the end of the city dock. "Hey, Shaina. We have to lighten the load."

She shoved her arms in the air like she didn't have a clue.

"I'm sending out the rowing team. Cast anything portable over the side of the barge to them. Look for anything that can lighten the load." The tug's diesel engines fell silent.

She cupped her hands to yell. "Like what? You want the kitchen sink out?"

Struck by the absurdity of her suggestion, he had to laugh. "Think smaller. What's left in the kitchen that a small boat could transport? Try cabinet drawers. We'll jettison the small stuff for starters, and then Dad is bringing the Coast Guard booms from Taylor Creek. If Reo can back the barge off the sandy bottom, we can run the barge's bow over the booms for extra floatation. Right now, the house is too heavy." A remembrance struck from nowhere. "How about all those seashells?"

She grabbed the sides of her face. "Oh, no. Not my knobbed whelks."

"Yes—throw them overboard to the rowing team for transport. We'll take care of them. Trust me." He balled up his fists and held them in the air to solidify his promise.

She disappeared under a panel of loose plywood inside the keeper's quarters.

Unsure the effort would be enough, he backpedaled down the dock. Off the far side of the barge, the first rowing scull reached its destination. Closer by, something knocked against the pilings beneath his feet.

"Hey, Mr. Landlocked," Jenna called with a teasing tone. "Want my boat?"

The answer made his shoulders shake as he withdrew his phone from his back pocket. "You bet. First, let me get a snapshot of this community effort. Talk about history unfolding." When she tossed the bow line onto the planks, he stepped on the rope and shot a rapid sequence of the armada arriving off the barge's laden bow. Ditching the phone, he jacked off his shoes and jumped into the water. By the time he'd surfaced, Jenna had climbed halfway up the ladder to the dock.

She glanced down grinning. "I hope this rescue confirms Beaufort as the best choice."

With a kick, he hauled his midsection over the gunwale and dropped into the bottom of the shallow hull. Once he'd righted on the seat, he claimed both oars and turned the bow. "Watch my phone, will you?"

"Hey, try to lend Shaina an encouraging word, little brother. Imagine her angst."

"Sky-high at that." With a nod, he headed straight for the jettison zone, wondering how many knobby seashells one racing scull could handle.

~

Exhausted, Shaina propped against the apothecary's porch post as the flatbed truck pulled away from the historic park, leaving the back half of the keeper's quarters sitting atop its new foundation. Though only partially completed, a small swell of satisfaction overwhelmed her hunger for the moment as she paused to take in the fitting permanent matchup.

Planking on the steps squeaked when someone approached behind her. She turned to find a sunburned but smiling veterinarian visiting her post. Too tired to pose an objection, she straightened to face him. "Hey, Judd. Thanks for everything today. Lightening the load was the right tactic. Please pass along my thanks to your dad, too. Those booms worked a miracle."

He ran a hand through his cropped hair. "Sure thing. We couldn't leave the barge stranded like that—not with our historical treasure still aboard."

She chuckled and gave the structure a final assessment. "Maybe the front section of the house will be lighter next trip. It mainly holds the stairway to the second floor."

"Dad has Mayor Wallace contacting the Corps of Engineers about the harbor dredging they've promised to schedule." He laughed and shook his head. "As it turns out, they're heading our way tomorrow with a side-cast dredge. Will wonders never cease?"

She appreciated all the special effort which made her job easier. Beaufort was filled with decent folks, after all. "Looks like the selection committee chose the right recipient site, today's sand-shoaled harbor notwithstanding."

His eyes sparkled with genuine emotion. "Shaina, I wish we could start all over again."

The flatbed truck gave a blast on its horn.

"Sorry, Judd. That's my cue to get going—or I don't have a ride back to Harkers Island for Round Two."

When she started off the porch, he caught her hand. "Let me drive you back. At least that would give me the chance to tell you what you really saw that night."

"Does it really matter in the long scheme of things? In two weeks, I'll be moving on to my next project." She tugged out of his hand and hurried down the stairs. Before he could object, she had the truck's passenger door open.

An inopportune moment, the truck driver startled and quickly hid a silver flask under his seat, gesturing for her to join him. A waft of hard liquor assaulted the humid evening. Before she could put a foot on the running board, her stomach growled a warning.

Without so much as a beckon, a peaceable perspective overrode the volatile situation. Shaina turned and regarded the earnest man still standing on the apothecary porch. Nearby, the din from an admiring public began to sound ethereal, a harmonic cadence. "Thanks, Joe, but I've decided to hang around town awhile. Someone else offered to run me back, so I'll see you Friday afternoon. Drive safely." She tossed him a wave as she slammed the door.

Within seconds, Judd's shoulder brushed hers. "Am I getting to drive you home?"

She raised a solitary finger in caution. "Only after we stop for a cheeseburger. I'm absolutely famished."

He chuckled while raising his arms over his head like a victor claiming the bout. "Make it a double-decker, and I'm definitely your man."

She stepped down the curb to cross the street to his clinic. Whether he won the designation of being *her* man remained to be seen. Still, the resourceful vet had a knack for rescue, that much could be written into the chronicles of history. She wouldn't miss the stench of diesel engines or Reo's constant flirting on the tugboat, for sure. The tipsy truck driver made for another questionable character in her final round of rescue, but enough drama had already played out for one day. That left her a juicy cheeseburger and one lame explanation away from a good night's rest. *What an exhausting ride, this historical preservation circuit.*

~

Rural Carteret County filled the windshield as the road to Harkers Island ran through low country replete with bridge crossings and crew-cut marshes scanned by their high-beam headlights. Judd knew his explanation bore missteps prior to his research involvement, but on Shackleford, they'd grown paramount—until the day Shaina fell into the inlet. Though Jenna's warning to sound contrite still burned his ego, being wrong differed from being sorry.

Shaina pointed toward the upcoming bridge. "Sure is low through here."

"I'm the lowest point on the map." He glanced her way and nodded. "Please let me get this off my chest. It's been a long, misdirected path I've traveled, but I wanted to lay out the truth for you. It involves the Shackleford Banks project, but that's not the entire issue."

She shifted toward him, crossing her arms. "Total truth then. I'm your captive audience."

The transition to the bridge's arch proved a perfect place to begin. "I call myself a shallow scoundrel, which I'm sure you would agree—but maybe not for the same reasons. I set lofty goals for vet school, but the program ranked high as a rigorous major. Duly challenged, I gave up all side pursuits to keep my focus and make good grades. That's when I adopted the mantra of *animals first*. Now, it seems like a ridiculous approach, but back then, the only people I took any interest in were the professors teaching my classes."

"What about after vet school when you set up your clinic?"

"Well, professionally I had to let people in at that point, as clients walk through the door almost hourly. Again, I could focus on my animal clients, tolerate the small talk, and build up my business. Jenna tried to get me active in the community with the hope I would meet someone to possibly date and fill out my *hollow shell* of a life. Her perspective, not mine."

"So the research project on Shackleford appealed to you. All animals and no people."

"Precisely, it held undeniable appeal for me. When the anonymous sponsor approached me with the offer to participate, I signed on then and there. Those two months on Shackleford collecting data brought me such a high level of satisfaction, I felt validated in my choices."

"So what happened to your smug satisfaction, Dr. Pearce?"

He drummed the steering wheel with his thumbs. *Total truth.* A quick glance in her direction lent him permission to continue. "You fell off your paddleboard in the middle of a ripping current. The moment I slung my frame off Thunder's back, my entire focus shifted. I'd seen you from afar a couple of times prior, but that day, you held my full attention. Your crisis called me out of my exclusive animal world and into turbulent waters. Guess I don't have to tell you, I'm still foundering in the shallows, tying to stay above water."

She braced her elbow on the console and leaned

toward him. "Tell me about the research project, as it seems to get between us more times than not."

"Fair enough. In the early nineteen eighties, the federal government set aside Shackleford Banks as a sanctuary to protect the resident wild ponies. You may have heard some of the stories about how that decision grieved the citizens of Harkers Island, a majority of whom kept summer houses out on Shackleford. To spite the government representatives, the men torched the summer houses when forced to abandon them, a tragic twist of fate. As it turns out, the wild ponies may have been a front used by federal entities to cover up another unaddressed matter."

"Like what?"

"Do you know the concrete bunker at the inlet on Cape Lookout?"

"Sure. I've been there a dozen times since it's not far from my beach grass planting."

"Similar in vintage—but not identical in function—Shackleford received its own outpost in the war, an ammo depot." When her eyebrows shot up into her hairline, he paused to take a deep breath. "Yes, it's what the locals call a war scab, and it still exists just west of Wade's Shore maybe a football field's length beyond the dock."

"You're kidding me, right?"

"I disclose this truth in all sincerity. The outer concrete casing has collapsed over time, but the subterranean pit they dug to hide the munitions remains intact. And it's tainted with chemical residue common to abandoned-in-place war facilities—mainly by benzene derivatives, as my specimens proved in the recent chemical analysis."

"Dear Lord. So the ponies coexist with the war scab, and the park service carries on like nothing's the matter. I'm absolutely incredulous over that resource conflict."

He snickered and wiped across his upper lip. "Must be a feminine reaction."

"Surely some of the fishermen knew about it?"

"Actually, you're not even close. Someone took note all right, but not the fishermen. Are you ready for this? The *women* of Harkers Island not only knew about it, but they came to me in search of a way to force some measure of rectification."

She gasped. "Do you mean the refreshment ladies?"

"Yep, meek and mild by every appearance, but they have a handle on the area's heritage and really showed some gumption to have the war scab examined."

"But why not let a sleeping dog lie?"

"Because the ponies are being affected by the seepage of chemical contaminants, that's why." He maneuvered the sharp turn where the road avoided an open cove. "The anonymous sponsor approached me, asking for a structured scientific experiment that could prove one way or the other that the two were not related."

"I'm not following you, Judd. Tell me. What two things are not related?"

"The war scab oozing its contaminants and the ponies' deformities. Their hooves are malformed—too straight. It affects their gait, even though they're mainly running through sand."

She dropped back against the seat. "God help us. This hurts to even hear about it."

"I got in over my head pretty quickly out there, living among the wild herd but having to measure contaminants. In late spring, I witnessed several spontaneously aborted fetuses, and suspected the ramifications went deeper than we first suspected. The future of the whole herd may be in jeopardy. That trend will take years to better document."

She held out a palm over the gear shift. "I can't take much more information. I simply can't. When I close my eyes, I just see the herd running across the dunes, wild and free."

"Please bear with me for one more disclosure. The day of the Morehead City public hearing for the keeper's quarters relocation, my results returned from the laboratory analysis. Shattering my null hypothesis that the war scar had no influence on the resident equines, the results showed contamination in every specimen I collected. The ponies all have some level of benzene in their tissues."

"Does that include my friend Stormy?"

"He's something to thank God for, as Stormy only possessed a trace of contaminant. Conversely, the veteran leader of the herd, Atlantica, had accumulations off the chart. In fact, he died from that war scab residue, I'm certain of it."

Shaina sat quietly as they crossed the county line headed into the boondocks. A solid five minutes passed with only the sound of exasperated exhalations. "So, if we're fully removing this misalignment between us, tell me who I saw in front of the clinic that night."

Breaking one truce to possibly gain another, he stared ahead into the nothingness. "That was the committee chairwoman, Nora Salter, the wife of ferry captain Gibbs Salter. She fell to pieces trying to get a grip on the magnitude of this indiscretion as I walked her out to her car. Somewhere, the damage has to stop. Part of that secrecy ends tonight with our conversation."

"So what kind of action will the women of Harkers Island take?"

"The legal kind, which should happen in short order. I remain on reserve as their expert witness. The lab results are compelling enough to force some manner of environmental remediation. I will simply read the data aloud in court and answer any technical questions."

"So, do you regret your involvement?"

"No, I remain resolute for justice, and demand a purified environment, should the ponies stay on Shackleford Banks. However, the research project did place me on a collision course with my misdirected path where animals came first. The war scab represented people, and that intermixed with the wild ponies. I faced a breaking point trying to rectify the interconnection—which is precisely when I ran into you."

Shaina chuckled under her breath. "No great wonder you tried to turn me into a mermaid that day. Animals first…and then you could doctor my head trauma without hesitation."

He shook his head at her deft assessment. "A wake-up call, for sure."

"I need…some time to sort through all this,

Judd. My top priority remains the relocation of the keeper's quarters. I'm compelled to finish this project. My future career hangs on it."

"You've got half a house settled in place, and half yet to go."

"Well, halves don't count in historic preservation—unless you want everything to end up cracked like the Liberty Bell."

He laughed at her analogy, though a deep fissure still existed between them. Maybe the truth could stitch them back together, though he wouldn't push for closure tonight. More pressing, the war scab had to fall into containment. Tonight, he'd tossed Shaina an olive branch. *Let it be enough.* The sign announcing Harkers Island graced the bridge support up ahead. One stop at park headquarters would surrender her to the opposition again, a fate of flat-out irony.

Chapter 10

Friday ended with the sweet sound of air compression as a nail gun sutured up the gaping mid-seam on two halves of the keeper's quarters. Seeing the entire building installed in a permanent home on the mainland, Shaina couldn't have been happier. The prim little park wrapped the new addition with a neatly mowed lawn while some elementary-aged children made a game of arranging the knobbed whelks around the building's new foundation.

Jenna appeared with a bowl of melting vanilla ice cream bearing a generous chocolate ripple. "Here's to landing a huge structure onto a welcoming landscape."

Shaina accepted the reward with a grin. "I was just having a similar thought. You know, outlining with seashells is something the lighthouse keeper's children would have done over a century ago."

"Funny how time can parallel like that, isn't it? Now, if you'll excuse me, I have to serve the other esteemed members of the relocation committee before Mayor Wallace bores them to death." She trotted back to the refreshment table as if to make good on the hasty delivery.

Judd waggled his brow while gesturing with his bowl. "Looks great, doesn't it?"

"The kids are being precious, playing with my seashells like that."

"Those little imps better keep them inside the park. We almost lost your precious cargo in the shallows. I toted at least two dozen in my scull while they tried their best to swamp me."

"Compared to the row team, your paddling looked amateurish."

"Okay. You're the one with the paddleboard, so hone my paddling skills. I beg you."

His personal request heated a rivulet up the side of her neck, as if August wasn't already steamy enough. "Well, Jenna is the rowing coach. Get her to teach you." She wanted to say something more personal, but the committee chairman headed right toward them. "Hey, Skip is coming our way. Try to be nice."

Instead of replying, Judd turned and held out his right hand for Skip to shake. "Here it is, sir, a done deal. Thank you for trusting us to have a lasting relationship with this weathered jewel from Cape Lookout."

Skip nodded and shook his hand. "We knew the wooden structure had to come off the island, as we couldn't keep up the necessary maintenance over there. It's simply too remote. Now, the lighthouse is another matter altogether. They sure built that tower to last."

She hummed in agreement. "Don't think I'll be signing up for that relocation job, should it arise. I might be headed up to New Jersey next. They're having chronic erosion up there that's threatening several historical structures."

Instead of adding any comment, Judd turned his spoon upside-down and devoured a glob of ice cream.

Skip stirred the melting puddle surrounding his scoop. "I think we'll plan to head back to Harkers Island in about fifteen minutes, Shaina, if you can finish up here and be ready to go." He followed with his classic watch-checking gesture.

"Sure thing. Let me get a few more pictures for my files. Meet you at the SUV."

After Skip walked off, Judd nudged her arm. "You don't have to go back tonight, Shaina. The apartment over the garage remains available for your use if you want to stay. Then you could get some pictures of the keeper's quarters in the morning light."

It hadn't occurred to her that most of her pictures would turn out dimly lit by the lateness of the hour. *Curse the complication.* "I'm trying to make the first ferry crossing out to Cape Lookout in the morning to post the bronze sign commemorating the original location of the keeper's house. That might represent a stretch driving from Beaufort."

"Nonsense. That's a ten o'clock departure, right? We could leave by eight-thirty and still be plenty early. I wanted to walk you down along the waterfront and show you the not-so-historical ruts your truck driver left when he took possession of the house earlier."

"Oops. I hope they aren't too noticeable." When

he hitched a cocky smile, she had to level with him. "Judd, listen. Strolling the waterfront sounds nice, but I'm not ready to stop at that gazebo with you. Looks like fate has us pointed in two different directions soon, and I don't want to generate any last-minute regrets."

"Fine. We'll only walk and talk. In the morning, I'll bring you a blueberry muffin, and we'll pause for a picture or three on our way out of town."

Her resolve melted at the suggested scenario. "You just had to throw in a blueberry muffin, didn't you?" Though he clamped his lips around the spoon, she didn't miss the sly wink. *Look at that.* Maybe the animal doctor could be cajoled out of the kennel, after all. That left her most of the night to decide whether she wanted to serve as the lure.

~

Seated in the ferry's stern beside Shaina, Judd hadn't missed the furtive looks from the fisherman in the bow. The lanky man clutched his fishing cooler like it held precious metal. Captain Salter had left the helm twice to corral a wayward kid from playing under the entry ramp's cordon rope. Otherwise, the crossing seemed routine.

Shaina shouldered into him. "Isn't that a royal tern? The one with the orange beak?"

"Yep, I think that's right. Good thing you're busy bird-watching, because someone else is plenty busy watching you."

"That's Reo Tillett, the tugboat operator. He's been a little too forward lately, yet another good reason to put Cape Lookout in my rearview mirror." She sighed and glanced along the marshes of Core

Banks. "Hope I remember only the good parts of this adventure." Her tone sounded wistful, like the distancing had already begun.

Captain Salter cleared his throat. "High tide lands around two o'clock. You don't want to be out on your paddleboard near the inlet 'round then."

Shaina smiled up at him. "No, sir. You know I enjoy a good slack tide when there's one to cross during the daytime. I respect the pull-and-push of the ocean, for sure."

Once the captain faded back to the wheelhouse, Judd leaned closer. "No ocean. Remember telling me that the first time?" He sweetened the probing question with a smile.

"What can I say? I fear my mother's retribution. I don't want to tell her any lies. Plus, I doubt my balance can handle those choppy waves."

"Sounds like another imbalance to me." Before he could wink, an explosion ripped across Core Sound, clapped his eardrums, and almost rocked the ferry. Protective, he clutched her in his grip. From the corner of his vision, he saw a fireball shoot skyward from the west. A plume of thick black smoke soon followed.

She broke away and stood to her feet. "What in the world?"

The captain approached in a hurry. "Sounded like cannon fire. Came from out on Shackelford Banks, I'm sure of that."

A knot formed in Judd's stomach. He rose on shaky knees. "I'm concerned about the ponies, Captain Salter. Do you think the ferry could run me over to Wade's Shore? I could make a quick check on the herd."

"Reckon I could. It's been awhile since I tried the dock at Wade's Shore though."

Shaina shot him a worried look. "I can bring the paddleboard over to find you after I'm finished over here on Lookout, Judd. I urge you to go find out what's happening."

The captain gave him a slight nod. "Give me five minutes to dock at Lookout so these day-trippers can get off. Then we'll head west to Shackleford...if they haven't blown the island to smithereens by then." Powerless, Gibbs threw up his hands and shifted back to the helm.

Judd glanced at the bronze plaque leaning against Shaina's backpack. "Okay, here's the plan. You head for the lighthouse and set the historical marker in place, get some pictures, and then pull the paddleboard out of storage. I'll expect to see you walking up the dune line on Shackleford in about an hour to join me. Does that scenario sound solid?"

She bit her lip, deep in contemplation. "Maybe an hour and a half, but certainly not two hours. A rising tide will advance through the inlet by then, but with the wind down, I don't expect any strong currents. I'm more afraid of what you might discover. If the herd happened to be standing near the explosion, you could find widespread carnage over there."

Seeing her bottom lip tremble, he sensed genuine trepidation which played against his heartstrings. "Don't worry about me. Vets are used to blood and guts, anyway." He ran a hand across her tanned forearm. "You can do me the biggest favor by making good time and arriving on my side early. Let's call it cooperative teamwork since you might have to help me shift the herd out of harm's way." He squelched the slight whimper she made with a hug he'd kept at the ready. As the diamond-spackled lighthouse appeared beyond the approaching dock, he caught the leering look from the fisherman standing in the bow.

∼

Shaina stepped out of the park service's restroom and knelt to pick up the paddleboard. After a short trek across the marsh road, she could put in south of the ferry landing and make for Shackleford Banks in record time. No doubt, Judd could use all the help he could muster. Partnering with another researcher seemed like a natural merger and brought a touch of healing, too. She extended the paddle to its full length and snapped the lock into place.

A double-rutted road leading to the ferry landing made for an effortless walk. She smiled, thinking Gibbs Salter practically kept that road from overgrowing by his constant driving around cape pointe. What a nice man to always check up on her like that before departing. *Yes, good memories.* She'd have to stroll past the Ammophila stand one last time for a reminder that small investments sometimes carried big payoffs when magnified by the passage of time.

She dropped the paddleboard beyond the marsh's edge and stooped to fit the ankle leash in place. To the south, the inlet appeared calm, unruffled by the tide switch. She'd made good time so far, which should please Judd when she walked up early on Shackleford's shore.

Commotion from under the ferry dock startled the pelican sitting atop a piling. From a hidden crouch Reo stood, stashing his cooler below the steps. "Hey there, Shaina."

Awkward as happenstance, she felt compelled to get out on the water and waded a step into the shallows. "Sorry, I'm off for a paddleboard outing, Reo. Good luck fishing back here."

Moving like lightning, he clamped a hand across her arm and jostled his body against hers. "No, I'm making my own good luck. And today I'm catching you, so forget about the paddleboard." As he tightened his grip, he stomped the SUP from her possession. "Play it my way and nobody gets hurt. Do you understand?" With a tug, he ripped the cord from her ankle.

"No, Reo. Keep your filthy hands off of me. I'm *not* going with you, so get that through your thick head." She pulled back, but not before the stench of beer on his breath drove the threat deeper. No wonder his cooler seemed so empty.

"How about we go for a little swim in the ocean off cape pointe?" Taking her arms, he forced her out of the safer sound waters. "I just don't get it. You know I have a soft spot for you, Shaina, but it seems like you're avoiding me or something." He dragged her onto the marsh road. "Today's our last day to celebrate the big relocation, so let's make it count, okay?"

"No. You and I have nothing to celebrate, Reo. If you weren't drunk, you'd recognize the truth."

She raised the paddle to push him away, but only managed to rile him.

He knocked the paddle to the ground. "Don't bother playing the too-good-for-you game." His tone turned bitter. "I see you're not too good for the pony doctor, so you're plenty good enough for me." As he shifted his grip, he caught a handful of hair and used the link-up to his immediate advantage. "All we need is a little shelter from full view, and then you're all mine."

She squeezed her eyes closed to recalibrate her mindset. After quick assessment, she spotted Barden's Inlet up ahead. That put cape pointe at a distance yet. Still, at this juncture, even the ocean's turbulence would be welcome. Maybe she could get away if a wave knocked Reo down. Plenty drunk, he couldn't be that coordinated.

He bumped her side, changing directions. "Not too far now, baby. Hang close to papa."

She convulsed at his use of pet names as she tried to keep pace. Otherwise, he'd pull out all her hair. Grass from the dunes soon tickled her legs as they began to ascend the rise toward cape pointe. Refracting off the ocean's solid blue, the hunkered concrete mass of the war bunker appeared directly ahead. *Dear God. Not our version of the war scar.*

Reo pulled something silvery out of his pocket that jangled in the sea breeze. "These might sweeten your attitude." With a lurid grin, he slapped a handcuff over her right wrist.

Stunned, she had to will her feet to walk. A prisoner now sentenced to the ultimate violation, she had to come up with a plan to stall this pervert.

Maybe with the sun's help, he'd pass out before inflicting any harm. Shifted askew by years of bludgeoning by the ocean, the bunker sat half buried by sand. To her horror, a breaking wave rushed into the open doorway, filling the bunker with roiling foam. *Curse the advancing tide.* She looked for something to leverage the scene in her favor, but the Ammophila grass stood too far out of reach.

~

Judd rubbed Thunder's mane and felt the horseflesh tremble beneath his touch. The herd members loitered off the dune ridge along the inlet, as far from the detonation crater as possible. For all he knew, their ears might still be ringing from the explosion.

By any reckoning, Shaina should have arrived by now. He'd scanned the horizon for her over half an hour ago, uneasy at the solo crossing. Not once had he spotted anyone out on the water. Odd that she wouldn't have started out by now, he sensed the need to close the gap between them. He clapped, hopeful to attract a partner. *Mackerel skies and stubborn ponies.*

When Stormy locked its knees, he waded out into the water alone and started splashing. "Come on out, boy. Let's swim the inlet. Think of all that lush green grass on the other side." Pressed by time, he soon relented to going unaccompanied and dipped into the inlet's flow. Assisted by the ease of the incoming current, he paced his stroke and labored for the far shore.

Near the halfway mark, he saw the pony abreast

of his location, swimming closer to the inlet. Something about the camaraderie struck an invisible chord, and the trip across became a tag-team effort. "Good Stormy," he called between breaths. Heartened, he quickened his pace and sailed through the remaining distance. At long last, one hand finally scraped bottom, so he lowered his legs and walked onto shore at Cape Lookout, his chest heaving.

The pony shook its mane and started toward the dune line along cape pointe. Instinctive, it headed for the beach grass patch on the island's interior. At the first big dune, it stopped and began pawing the ground.

Winded from the swim, Judd broke into a slow jog to examine the object of the animal's gesturing. He crested the height of the dune and spotted what looked like a discarded beach towel at first glance. With a nudge of the pony's muzzle, the heap gave a low moan. He caught a faint whiff of beer. *Intoxicated, huh?* An instant recollection, he recognized the swim trunks of the leering fisherman from the ferry. Sunburned and looking worse for wear, he decided to leave the hapless drunk alone to sober up. Ever more urgent, he needed to find Shaina.

A substantial wave crashed nearby on the beachfront, followed by the cry of a seagull. When Stormy came charging past, he reevaluated the piercing cry and headed for the shore. A bulky concrete structure sat half-sunken in sand, pummeled nonstop by the incoming tide. Another cry went up as the foamy wave rushed into the bunker. Stormy stopped short of the entrance, planting its front legs wider against the rushing water.

He approached with dread, bending below the upper concrete slab. "Shaina?"

"Help me…I'm trapped…"

Another wave broke and rushed into the relic before he could respond. From the bunker's angle of collapse, high tide would soon fill up the concrete box, leaving no space for air. He fought the refracting wave's tug to stride into the bunker, straining to see further inside. Something dark moved along the right wall. "Wait. I see you. Give me a sec to get over there."

"Hurry, before the next wave. I can't breathe when the water floods in. Reo handcuffed me to an iron ring so he could attack me."

Digging his toes into the sand to leverage against the current, he reached her and assessed the situation. He wiped the hair from her face. "Hang with me, okay. I've got to break this ring." As a wave rushed into the interior, he tucked her head into the crook of his neck for protection. At the height of the wave's rush, they had four inches of airspace remaining, at most. He fingered the loop of the handcuff, built solid to resist the strongest protest. *No go.* He'd have to loosen the iron ring from the wall instead.

Once the wave retreated, he pulled the knife out of his belt and used the sharp point to chip away the weathered mortar. His desperate scrapes made little progress. He stopped and sheltered her as another wave tried to drown them.

After the wave ebbed, Shaina spit and tried to clear her lungs. "Thank the Good Lord you're here, Judd. I kept begging God to send you, and he did."

"Let's hold that thought to savor later. Right now, I need a better strategy than carving out this mortar. Are you hurt?"

"No. Reo staggered out after I fought him off. He left and never came back." She tucked into his neck voluntarily as the next wave assaulted the bunker with a thunderous roar.

Judd knew he held precious cargo. Now, he needed to free her from being bound and escape the death cave at high tide. The refracting current threatened to pull them apart, but he resisted. Ready to try anything, he slipped his thumb inside the handcuff ring to check the tautness. *Wiggle room, but not enough.*

The empty cuff banged against his forearm, gleaming silver in the dim light. His school chum always had a trick ready with handcuffs, but that guy was double-jointed. Suddenly, his anatomy knowledge pulsed to the forefront of his scheming, an occupational asset. With it, he sensed a way out. "Listen. We're running out of air here in the bunker. I'm going to break the hold the handcuff has on your wrist, but it's going to hurt like mad for a split second."

Her startled gaze searched his face. "What? Don't cut me with that knife. Please, Judd, think of something else."

An incoming wave left him no time to second guess. "Grab onto me. We're riding out with the ebbing current." Before the wave could advance, he turned the knife hilt-down and smashed the heel of her thumb with a forceful blow. Once the digit broke from place, he eased her limp hand through the narrow cuff. The refracting wave silenced her scream, so he gathered her in his arms and rode the outgoing current toward the openness of unhindered daylight.

Stormy nickered at his approach and then scampered as a taller figure cast a shadow across the bunker's entrance.

His back to the ocean, Reo brandished a small handgun. "Not so fast, pony doc."

Judd caught a glimpse of the drunk's sand-covered hands and sensed an advantage. He shoved Shaina toward the pony and dove for the weapon. The next wave crashed and flushed past them, knocking them both to the ground. He wrested the handgun free and pitched it out into the ocean. Pumped by adrenalin, he pinned the drunk underwater and freed up his own weapon.

Once the water cleared, he dragged Reo higher onto the beach letting his blade glimmer in the broad sunlight. "Haven't you ever heard, punk? Never bring a gun to a knife fight." With a flick of his wrist, he slit the man's swim trunks down the side seam. "That's how I prep for a neutering job. Now you tell me, should I finish the operation?"

Reo held up both palms in surrender. "Lay off, man. I came down to fish the cape. That's all—no harm done."

Judd backed off, making a slicing gesture through the air. The sound of sobs drew him to where Shaina stood with Stormy. Thinking she might have a different explanation, she gained his undivided attention. After lifting her in his arms, he placed her across the pony's back and led them both toward the dune line. Her whimpers tore a jag across his heart, but now they were free to live and love, starting from Lookout's infamous cape pointe. Hunkered above the island's vista, the diamond-clad lighthouse rotated a glimmer of light as if to appease a sailor in peril.

"Come hold me, Judd." A sob followed Shaina's request.

He dropped back and laced his arm across her shoulder. "How was that for a broken pledge salvaged at the last possible second, Miss Gillespie?" When her sobs yielded to a tiny chuckle, he brushed his cheek against hers. A car horn sounded from the marsh road. "Well, if it isn't your old watchdog coming to offer us a lift. Maybe we should swap vehicles and let the pony graze in the Ammophila for a bit."

"That's a strong maybe, Dr. Pearce, but not exactly animals first."

"No." He paused to deliver a contrite kiss on her salty lips. "I like my new tactic better." With that admission, he scooped her off the pony's back to take full possession of his treasure. In steps, the pony veered off toward the beach grass patch as anticipated. "Go your own way, Stormy. I'm holding the real nirvana."

The dune buggy pulled astride, looking less rusted out than he remembered. Though cape pointe maintained its stronghold on the island, he'd upheld the *no ocean* restriction for one final round. No more thundering waves threatened their togetherness. Instead, he'd settle for a favorable crossing current to navigate safely back to the mainland.

Epilogue

Not quite a month into her new job, Shaina admitted the situation suited her to perfection. She shined the brass doorknob of the apothecary shop with her left hand while her right hand rode limp in a sling. Next door, the lighthouse keeper's quarters sat repaired and ready for duty. After Labor Day weekend, she would host countless tours for all the elementary classes eager to learn about local history.

A car pulled up to the curb. "Hey, Shaina," Judd called. "Can you quit ten minutes early today? I've found something promising I want to show you."

She tucked her rag under the top step and traipsed down the steps to meet him. "You aren't going to show me those truck ruts again, are you?"

He shook his head. "No, something better, Scout's honor."

She opened the passenger door and hopped inside. "Historians love a touch of intrigue, you know. It makes the rendering of events so much more compelling."

"This is the land of pirates, so you're in the right place." He floored the accelerator and headed north out of town. Once they passed the highway, he relaxed behind the wheel. "I want you to look at my latest opportunity. It's not really veterinarian work, or even scientific inquiry."

"Okay, and I'm guessing it's not historical either. Am I right?" She rolled her window down and braced her sling against the air flow.

"Well, I'm sure it has a bit of history involved, since the location flanks Harlowe Creek." Within minutes, he slowed the vehicle to a crawl. "Note the fence line starting here at this corner." They eased up the road as the loveliest meadow opened along the coast.

"Wow. This is truly picturesque—out in the country with no noise or hint of pollution." She took a deep breath. "The air even smells better out here."

Judd gave a little smile and steered the car up a dirt driveway, stopping at a bank of overgrown shrubs. "Let me introduce you to the Baker homestead. Dad claims Mr. Baker moved away last year to live with his son in Arizona. He's just now putting the property on the market. Gonna be a great deal for somebody, so I thought we should come take a look." He gestured at the windshield and got out of the car.

She joined him and discovered the quaint coastal cottage hiding in the overgrown foundation plantings. A porch covered the front of the house. "Oh, my. This house is darling."

"Wait until you see out back. The property comes with several sheds and a chicken coop." He led around the nearest corner and beckoned for her to join him.

She strode through the tall grass and saw an old-fashioned clothesline flanking the back porch. Flowerbeds lined the path to the main outbuilding. The chicken coop's gate hung open, making her wonder how long it had stood empty.

"So what do you think?"

"I'm not sure yet. How big is this property?"

"Twenty-five acres, more or less. The house has two bedrooms and one bath. The realtor lamented that no remodeling has been done to date." Seeming restless, he wandered off toward a larger enclosure.

Too many unanswered questions flooded to mind. She rubbed shoulders with him along a corral railing. "What aren't you telling me, Judd Pearce?" Before he could answer, a small pony stepped out of the shed and trotted toward her. A shiver of recognition shot across her shoulder blades. "How could? Is that Stormy? What on earth is he doing here?"

Judd flashed a lopsided grin. "He's recovering in an untainted pasture. We have enough room here for three to four more Shackleford ponies—if we want more."

"We do? And who's going to decide how many?" Stormy came to the fence and nuzzled her arm. Too tenderhearted to resist, she rubbed the pony's muscular neck.

"Well, Skip Reeder put in a good word for me as an adoption host before he left the area. Guess you could say he blasted his way out of the park service into early retirement."

She shook her head. "None of this makes any sense to me. Is there something you're not telling me?"

He took her hand and then dropped to one knee. "I don't need to tell you anything more than this—you make every day seem special when you spend time with me. I want more of that togetherness, like a lifetime more." He paused long enough to reach for something in his shirt pocket. With an insistent wiggle, he held a glittery solitaire next to her ring finger. "Shaina Gillespie, Would you marry me? You'd have my whole heart all the days of my life."

"Does that come with a promise of no more secrets?" She pretended to retract her hand.

Judd held fast. "No secrets, and no more half-witted aims. Only togetherness." When Stormy nickered, he tilted his head to one side. "And maybe a handful of animals close by."

"Then yes, I would love to be your wife, Doctor Judson Pearce. I hope you're planning to show me inside this darling house next. I might need to improve some structural features."

He stood and took her into his arms. "Oh, no. Here we go again."

Shaina snuffed out his protest by matching her lips to his. Faster than crossing a bridge and easier to maneuver than a barge, she made the memorable link-up count for the history books. *What God hath joined together, let no man put asunder.* While their embrace lingered, Stormy began to paw at the bottom rail, ready to run wild and free inside their pristine coastal pasture.

The End

Enjoy this peek at Salt-Stung on Cape Hatteras

Chapter 1

The shoals running off cape pointe sucked the life out of terra firma, but no one ever came to Hatteras to gawk at underwater elevations. No, Jaima Delarie knew better. They came to fish. October ramped up angler excitability. Bluefish would start running the inlet any day now.

With the tide ebbing, the ocean pulled at her ankles as if to insist on her departure. One glance at the two shrimp left in her bait box argued against that brash tactic. Unfortunately, those thawing crustaceans would keep her brooding out in the intertidal zone through dead slack tide, most likely. If that yielded her one fresh fish to cook for dinner tonight, she could justify the time. *C'mon. One measly Spanish mackerel, Lord.*

The daring peninsula of sand chopped the oceanic currents like atmospheric turbulence battling for supremacy. Rising tide quelled the aqueous fight to encompass dry land, but an ebb tide lacked strength to sort out such matters. Her life had taken on the illusion of a falling tide lately. She reeled in her line to find her leader affixed with a dangling triangular weight and a bare hook. "Minus one shrimp and counting."

As she baited the hook, a powder-blue motorboat passed heading inland. The crossing of Pamlico Sound took the better part of half an hour, even under mild winds. The channel markers would be blinking back darkness by then. Anguished at not having caught dinner, she wiped her hand dry and cocked the surf rod back to cast.

Instinctive, she checked the pole's tip for a fouled line and caught a glimpse of the iconic Hatteras lighthouse, its shadow marking the dunes like a sundial. She let the cast rip from the strength of her shoulders. Told she bore a sturdy build by those who knew her best, she put her six-foot frame to work and cleared the shore break by twice the needed distance. A positive sign, the shrimp stayed connected to the bottom rig and made the plunge into the salty Atlantic.

The following lull snapped on a seagull's cry and an odd throttling noise that ended in a hollow thump. A scan of the eastern shoreline yielded one slightly imperiled vessel listing to port and badly aligned for an emergency landing. No one in their right mind beached a watercraft along the shore, as ocean waves could swamp any rookie attempts at dry-land safety. To prove the point, a rolling swell crested against the bow of the boat, an enticing lick of disaster.

Her pulse elevating, she shoved the handle of the fishing pole into the nearby rod holder and sidestepped like a scuttling crab toward the disabled craft. The throttle noise repeated, followed by a metallic clank. When the boat captain threw his arms over his head, the icy drip of peril seized her chest. *Graveyard of the Atlantic repeats its claim.*

Underpowered to manually prevent the landing, she reasoned the last dune buggy had left the beach almost an hour ago. Maybe they should attempt to minimize the damage. She cupped her hands around her mouth to amplify her message and feign a steady calm. "Can you throw your anchor and drag a line to slow down?"

"Dragging two anchors already," the captain replied. "I'm jettisoning cargo. Watch for it." A swell passed, crowning as it approached shore. Two red coolers soon bobbed in the gray-blue waters. Buoyant, they floated in when the next wave crashed onto the wreck scene.

Despite the resisting anchors, all else seemed to morph from impossible rescue to imminent salvage. Jaima drew her cell phone and pressed a familiar number for help. When the line opened, she made it quick. "I've got a boat in peril off cape pointe. She's coming in and nothing's gonna stop that collision. Can you bring the Suburban over?"

"Be right there," a brusque voice replied. "You save the captain—I'll get the boat."

She shirked out of her windbreaker, knotted the sleeves around her phone, and tossed it onto the upper shore for safekeeping. "Sure, give me the easy-breezy job." One glance at her stock-still rod yielded no further excuses. She had to lend aid.

Within seconds, the first cooler rode a breaker into the shallows, so she waded out to retrieve it. Riding low in the rushing water, she figured fish weighed the box, suggesting the captain might not be a total incompetent. The drag to shore strained her back muscles, but she bent her knees and gave the effort all she had. A repeat trip for the matching cooler proved equally arduous. She rested above the wrack line left by the earlier high tide and watched the captain toss the last of several smaller bundles into the ocean.

A cataclysmic battle ensued between twin-rigged anchors and Mother Nature. The vessel's stern soon became ill-matched for the tidal influence of the moon's gravitational pull. A large swell crested directly into the boat and emptied. Doomed, the craft sunk to half-mast.

A growl emanated from atop the far gunwale as the captain refused to go down with the ship. In a splash, the Atlantic swallowed the man whole. Its salt-gray waters turned murderous.

Jaima scanned the beachfront from the rolling swells to the shore break. The barrier islands of North Carolina wore the rescue of imperiled ships like a badge of folklore courage. Unfolding in live action, the perilous scene felt more like a tourniquet tightening around her throat. Twice she spotted a dark-haired crown in the surface chop, only to lose sight of the floundering man in the next frothy wave.

A handful of breakers swamped the boat, and its hull began scraping the sandy bottom. Kept from going broadside to the surf, the twin dragging anchors saved the boat, a fated twist of seamanship that kept the barrage of waves from outright demolishing the small vessel.

When a horn sounded from the dune crossing,

her rescuer's trip from Hatteras bight came full circle back to cape pointe. Only partially relieved, she crouched in the shallows to minimize the setting sun's glare and tried to locate the victim while the Labrador Current chilled her legs. A dash of plaid shimmered close by, so she trotted out for immediate retrieval. Waiting out the next crashing wave, she waded deeper and squinted to remedy refraction at the water's surface. This time when she spotted plaid, she lunged to make a frantic grab and connected.

A Herculean grasp responded to her touch as a roller broke with a roar. Enveloped in saltwater spray, his arms clutched her trunk and two figures became one under the wave's thunderous christening. Toppled by the wave's power, a confused sense of uprightness gave way to a flushing tumble toward shore. A mix of sand, icy water, and sea foam further convoluted her senses. Deprived of air, her lungs began to burn. At last the waters receded, allowing the upper shore to win.

Monte squatted over them with a belly-shaking chuckle. "That there's one way to land 'em, missy. Let's get the boat out before it fills up with sand and strains my wench. Can one of you castaways find your land legs?"

A pair of mesmerizing hazel eyes shot open at the mention of the boat. His hand rubbed a plaster of wet sand off a tanned cheek. "Lord on earth. What just happened?"

She shoved out of his clasping arm and rolled back to retake her feet. In a squat, she regarded the wreck-prone captain as water dripped from her jeans. "You just missed Hatteras Inlet by approximately two hundred feet."

He moaned and tried to sit upright in the sand. "Not sure if I ran out of gas or the engine failed. Either way, a miss is as good as a shipwrecked mile."

Monte pointed at him. "You come up front and help keep the bow centered on the rollers. Del-doll, you take the bailer and rid excess weight from the hull as best you can." He tossed her the scoop and made for the cab of the Suburban.

Jaima walked out on wet sand exposed by a dead slack tide and rued the happenstance. Bailing the almighty Atlantic out of a skiff's hull stacked the deck toward impossible yet again. Behind the sulking hull, two taut anchor lines trailed seaward like contrails tracing some ill-chosen path. *The men can fetch those tethered beasts.* With a heave of her shoulders, the first scoop of sand and water regained its home off cape pointe.

AUTHOR BIO

A coastal North Carolina native, Cindy M. Amos writes fiction about conflicts of man living on the land from her outpost in Wichita, Kansas. Holding an advanced degree in coastal marine biology, she spent two years on Cape Lookout researching the effects of dune buggies on the island's topography and vegetation. Sleeping on the sand under the lighthouse's constant beacon, she gained a unique perspective on the island's isolating dynamic. Proud to have partnered with the park service and met uncountable day-trippers to the remote beach during her studies, she now delivers this authentic tale of current-ripped barriers and confused allegiances where fragile romantic ties face the ultimate test of durability.

"Current-Ripped on Cape Lookout" represents the author's 41st book with Editor Cynthia Hickey at Winged Publications, a small traditional publisher out of Surprise, Arizona.

Member: American Christian Fiction Writers and

Heart of America Christian Writers Network.

Her entire booklist with Winged Publications can be found on her website:
  http://cindymamos.wixsite.com/natureink

Her author page on Amazon is found at:
  https://www.amazon.com/Cindy-M.-Amos

~Writing romance onto nature's landscape~

OTHER BOOKS BY CINDY M. AMOS
Landscapes of Mercy Series
Redeeming River Rancher
Saving Bicycle Man
Justifying Sound Strider
Sanctifying Ace Aerialist
Lifting Lock Runner
Salvaging Doctor Junk

National Parks 100th Anniversary Romance Collection
Everglades Entanglement
Mesa Verde Meltdown

Holiday 3-in-1 Collection
Running Out of Christmastime

Taming the Cowboy's Heart Collection
Warming Stone Cold Lodge

50 States Collection
Secondhand Flower Stand (Kansas)

Red Cloud Retreat (Nebraska)
Tidewater Lowlands (North Carolina)
Canyon Country Courtship (Utah)

John Denver 20th Anniversary Collection
Calypso Reimagined

Loving the Town Hero Collection
Cascading Waterworks

Cowboy Brides Collection
Renegade Restoration

America's Fabulous Fifties Series
Oil Field Maven
Airfield Aptitude
Camp Field Capable

Small Town Christmas Collection 2018
Gift Tag Tree

Romancing the Rancher's Daughter Collection
Waylaying the Hauler

Romancing the Farmer Collection
Furrowed Hearts

Adventure Brides Collection
Ocean's Edge

Romancing the Bachelor Collection
Impasse to Springtime

Romancing the Boy Next Door Collection
Forty Acres on Loan

Romancing the Doctor Collection
X-Raying the Doctor

Vote for Love Collection
Ballot Box Rumors

A Secret Santa Romance Collection
Sweet Regrets from Sourwood

Christmas Cookie Brides Collection
Pizzelles for Elves

Romancing the Drifter Collection
Derailing the Drifter

A Family to Love Collection
Skinny Ranch Romance

Nonfiction Little Lift Gift Books
Signs of the Seasons: Hints from Nature

The Men of Mustang Pass Series
Silver Lining at Mustang Pass
Copper Halo at Mustang Pass
Sapphire Skies at Mustang Pass
Holiday Hitches at Mustang Pass

Horizons of Hidden Promise
Rekindled from Ashes
Reconciled from Heartache